The Last Rider from Hell

Staked out under the baking heat of the desert sun by Frank Chapel's riders from hell is no way for any man to die. Only someone as resilient as Matt Travis had the courage to endure the heat, the vultures and survive. When finally he manages to escape a gruesome death only one thing is on his mind – revenge.

But his memory has been blasted to oblivion and he is even unsure of his own name. All he knows is that everyone wants him dead!

Justice must be done and Matt will be judge, jury and hangman. First, though, he must face up to the truth of his past and, that accomplished, lead begins to fly.

The Last Rider from Hell

I.J. PARNHAM

A Black Horse Western

ROBERT HALE · LONDON

© I.J. Parnham 2002
First published in Great Britain 2002

ISBN 0 7090 7043 8

Robert Hale Limited
Clerkenwell House
Clerkenwell Green
London EC1R 0HT

Typeset by
Derek Doyle & Associates, Liverpool.
Printed and bound in Great Britain by
Antony Rowe Limited, Wiltshire

ONE

The vultures were closer now.

In an unending barrage, the sun beat down its merciless heat on to the rock-filled Utah desert.

Beneath the inferno, a man lay spread-eagled, facing upward. Thick bonds tied his hands and feet to heavy stakes driven deep into the unforgiving desert. Each stake was set far enough apart to hold and stretch him without hope of escaping.

With his head turned as far as possible from the blinding rays of the sun, the man's cheeks and neck still fried. He couldn't shield his face as the sun burned him to death in the slowest way possible.

Yet again, the man tried to drag his arms upward. His arms stayed down.

How long he had been here, the man didn't know. He was aware of a yesterday and perhaps a day before that. Before then, his thoughts refused to travel. The sun had fried his mind and he couldn't remember anything more.

What had he done to deserve suffering this slow death? Who had staked him here?

The answers were beyond remembering.

Worse, the man didn't know his own name.

With the sun rising in the sky, he knew these worries wouldn't last much longer. Before long, the sun would blind him and then bake him. By sunset, his last duty would be to feed the vultures that circled ever closer.

Without much hope, the man flexed his arms, but he was too weak to know if he moved them.

While the man kept his eyes closed to preserve his eyesight, the great birds flapped around him. The man believed dead meat attracted them, so they wouldn't attack him while he lived. Then again, they wouldn't need to wait much longer.

Amid the cawing of the squabbling birds, flies buzzed. They crawled over his exposed skin as they staked their claim for this piece of fresh meat before the vultures took their share.

Wings flapped. A shadow covered the man's face. With this momentary respite from the sun, he opened his eyes.

A vulture hulked over him. Its beak was open wide in anticipation.

The reek of death surrounded him.

Despite his baked throat, a cry loosened itself from the man's chest.

In surprise, the vulture squawked away from him. Then with a crash, which shook the man's body, it flew into the stake pinning his right arm.

For terrible seconds, the man's body racked apart. The pressure almost wrenched his arm from the socket. Then the pressure yielded.

The man sighed gratingly. He only had hours left but the vultures wouldn't take him while he lived. He flexed his arm. It was less constrained than before.

Supposing the vulture had done more damage than he had previously thought, the man looked to his right. The stake holding his right arm was at a sharp angle to the rocky ground. The huge bird, in crashing into the stake, had partially dragged it from the ground.

Gulping in his dry throat against the hope that hit him, the man flexed his arm, testing whether the stake was loose enough to move. His bones creaked as he moved them for the first time in days.

The stake moved six inches.

The man reached the extent of his movement to the right, paused, and then moved his arm in the opposite direction. His arm moved six inches in that direction too. Better, the stake creaked as much as his arm did.

Wasting no time on wondering if he could escape, the man pushed his arm upward. In a pebble-filled shower, the stake surged from the ground and his arm thrust into the air above his head.

The man grinned, but with the first possibility of escape, his heart raced in panic. When staked in the desert, he'd die. Now with a hint of hope, he flexed his arm.

He forced his shoulder upward and at the extent of his reach, he wrapped his free hand around the stake holding his left arm. Then he fell back; in another creaking shower of pebbles, the stake slipped from the desert ground.

The man pushed himself to a sitting position. He stretched his sore back as far as possible and grabbed the stake holding his left leg. He tugged backward. When the stake failed to move, he lurched to his right and with a firm grip, pulled the right stake clear.

Now that he was almost free, he shuffled towards the final stake, wrapped both arms around it and pulled it loose. Then he pushed to his feet and stood, swaying back and forth.

With the stakes still attached to his ankles and wrists, he staggered to the nearest boulder and fell into a rare piece of shade. Despite the oppressive heat, here was a small pool of coolness. With his legs drawn to his chest, he wondered what he could do.

The man had no idea as to his current location, or the direction of safety. If he were near to a town or a commonly used trail, someone would have found him, so he must be many miles from help.

Despite his poor memory, he knew that travelling at night was the safest way of walking through a desert, but in his present weak state, he doubted he'd be alive by sunset.

Without a choice, he dragged the stakes from his limbs, staggered to his feet, and stumbled into the raging heat.

The flies buzzed again, dense and insistent.

As the man rounded the boulder, he smelt the rank odour and knew what he'd see before he reached the other side.

Staked on the ground ten yards before him were three fly-blown bodies.

Vultures squabbled over the bodies. The birds turned their vast heads to the man and shuffled back a few feet to wait for the interruption to end.

The man staggered forward to stand over the bodies.

The first person had died from repeated, frenzied stab wounds. A dagger still protruded from the body's chest.

Stakes secured the second person's body across the chest and thighs. With a grimace, the man noticed the victim's hands and feet lay in a pile a few yards away.

The third person appeared to lack skin.

Each of these people had died an increasingly painful death. The man gulped drily. He wondered if an interruption had stopped their torturers before they perpetrated whatever painful end they'd intended for him. If the third person's fate were a guide, the death they'd planned for him was horrendous.

The man sighed. The death they'd planned for him *was* the worst of all. They'd let him live to die the slowest of deaths.

The man turned from the corrupted bodies. He shielded his eyes as he examined the barren, white-glowing desert. He discovered that he was on a small plateau, facing a gully, which nestled between two steep-sided hills. Beyond, the landscape was empty of features.

He turned around. In all directions, the rock-strewn surface was unrelenting and free of any vegetation or sign of civilization. The only movement came from the vultures that circled over the gully.

With no clue as to how he might escape, he pondered. All directions appeared to lead to death. In which direction he wanted to meet that death was his only choice.

For long minutes, the man found nothing to guide him. Then his gaze became accustomed to the harsh terrain.

Trails coated the ground a few yards from him. Having identified the scuffed markings, he found hoof-prints lying around the staked men. They led beyond another rock pile and down into the gully.

With his direction resolved, the man let the vultures return to their interrupted feast and staggered down this trail and into the gully. Towering rocks loomed over him as he stumbled and slid down the gully side.

At the bottom, bodies lay everywhere. They sprawled over the remnants of a small wagon train.

The six half-burnt wagons were in a defensive circle. The swath of death around them showed that the defenders had failed.

With flies filling the air, the man staggered forward. He wandered from body to body searching for someone who might still be alive. Everywhere he looked, the ravaged bodies had been dead for days.

He counted twelve bodies, including women who had died beside their men. Too much time had passed to suggest who these people were when alive. As gunshot burns holed their clothing, the cause of their deaths was clearer.

The man looked in each wagon. Within the third,

three children huddled in the corners. They were dead too.

'They didn't need to do that,' the man mumbled, and with these croaked words, he remembered how dire his situation was.

He searched for food and water. Beside a wagon he found a barrel with a gunshot hole half-way down one side. He threw the barrel top to the ground. His own dishevelled sunburned reflection stared back. With a grating whoop of joy, the man thrust his head into the barrel and gulped down water until he choked. Then with the barest pause for breath he plunged his head back in to gulp again.

With his imminent survival assured, the man planned how to prolong his luck. Further investigation yielded no help. His riffling through clothing and the wagon remnants failed to reveal a map. The two remaining horses were dead and food was only noticeable by its absence.

When the sun edged close to the horizon, the man decided.

He gulped as much water as he could stomach and filled the two canteens he'd found. Then he upended the water barrel over his head. Without a backward glance, he marched down the wheel-rutted trail the wagon train had taken to reach this terrible place. The wagons had come from somewhere. His only hope was to retrace their journey and hope he'd find safety before his water ran out.

The man walked from the gully. He passed a formation of rocks shaped like a lizard then faced the flat desert terrain. The setting sun threw his long shadow out before him. Ahead, the wagon-trail stretched. To the north were low hills. To the south was endless light sand.

When the sun set his clothes were already dry and returned to their previous gritty state. Afterwards the temperature plummeted. With the coolness and water in his belly, the man was happier with his predicament.

Maintaining his eastward direction, he walked through the night. For company he had the wheel markings running across the sand below him, and, above him, the harshly bright stars. Every hour he stopped to empty his boots of sand, but as the sky lightened he no longer bothered.

An hour after sunrise he sheltered next to a large rock outcrop. Huddled in the coolness, he slept while the sun did its worst.

At sunset he walked again, although the trail was hard to follow. The slight breeze blowing in his face shifted the sand over the wheel-markings.

Even with rationing, his first canteen ran out during the second morning of his journey. The second canteen yielded its last precious drop of water on the third afternoon.

Then all the man had left was his willpower.

He maintained his general eastward direction, receiving no encouragement from the stars shining down on him.

He walked throughout the fourth night, without sign of civilization or water. In the morning, he searched for shelter and then stopped. Without water for two days and food for over a week, he was beyond weakness. Only his legs' refusal to stop moving kept him walking.

If he stopped, he'd never start again.

He knew deserts often trapped their few visitors with mirages. As the morning heat built to the unforgiving inferno of midday, he experienced them.

The outline of buildings shimmered in the distance. Seemingly, he'd been walking by them for years.

The wheel-trails beneath his feet were no longer there. They hadn't been for a long time.

The man stumbled to his knees and tottered back and forth. He was torn between accepting that the buildings existed and so walking to them, and believing them a mirage and so falling on to the sand and dying.

If they were a mirage, he was only wasting his time in living for a few more minutes.

The man decided to waste that time.

He staggered to his feet and aimed for the buildings, shuffling forward painfully. Each step he dragged from his faltering legs didn't bring the buildings closer. Just as he decided they were a figment of his sun-blasted imagination, a fence appeared before him.

With a tentative hand, the man closed his fingers on the rough lumber. He ran his hand along the fence. The wood grated his fingertips. This was the first object that he'd felt for a while that wasn't sand or rock. Now knowing that the town wasn't a mirage, he ducked through the fence-posts and staggered to the buildings.

A few yards on, he reached a sign.

'HELL'S END. POPULATION 47,' the sign proclaimed.

'Wrong, forty-eight,' the man mumbled, and pushed on to the buildings.

A few rough adobe buildings were on either side of the only road. Some buildings had signs above their doors offering such delights as a saloon and stores. The man staggered to the nearest building, the saloon. He stumbled on to the short porch, through the swing-doors, and into the coolness beyond.

While the flies buzzed, he swayed in the entrance. His eyes refused to focus on the gloom inside. Then he saw people. In relief, he fell to his knees.

On the sandy floor, he forced his head up.

Three men lined the back wall, leaning back in their chairs with hats pulled low over their faces. A bearded man loomed over him.

'Please,' the man said in a croaking whisper with a hand over his brow. 'Help me. I need water.'

The bearded man smiled. He pulled a gun from its holster and pointed it at the man.

'I had a feeling you'd return,' he muttered. 'You should have stayed where you were.'

TWO

Sheriff Cassidy Yates sat tall in his saddle and wiped a hand over his sweating brow. After two months of travelling from Abilene, he was a long way from the lush Kansas prairies that he loved. On the Utah border, barren desert faced him, stretching ahead seemingly without end.

Nathaniel McBain, his fair-haired young deputy, matched Cassidy's hand-rub across his forehead.

'I don't like the look of this,' Nathaniel said with a long sigh.

As the heat had battered Cassidy's desire to chat from him, he nodded.

Two months ago, he'd eagerly accepted this first assignment as a sheriff, but faced with the reality, he wasn't so pleased any longer. The assignment didn't worry him, but leaving the prairies he'd spent his life in didn't fill him with enthusiasm.

Over the last year, three wagon trains that had left Kansas and headed west to California hadn't arrived at their intended destination.

Only yesterday they'd learned that a fourth wagon

train, Matt Travis's, was late arriving at an expected stop in Nevada.

On the route, the wagons could meet an unfortunate end in many ways. The desert that Cassidy now approached was the first possible candidate and to his way of thinking, the most likely. His nagging doubt was that a journey across a desert might account for the occasional disaster. Four failures suggested that humans and not nature might prove to be the culprits.

So, two lawmen protected the latest wagon train. If he and Nathaniel didn't discover the fate of the previous wagon trains they would return to Beaver Ridge and accompany the next one. Afterwards they would continue escorting wagon trains until they *did* discover what had happened. This last fact convinced Cassidy that he must discover what was happening this time.

A few hundred yards ahead, the wagon train had stopped.

Cassidy sighed. They had only travelled for two hours this morning. Aside from the heat, the other matter he disliked about this journey was the slow pace of travel. Any excuse to stop was a good reason for these pioneers. As usual, the blank terrain provided no reason for this stoppage.

Keeping his distance to avoid the pioneers dragging him into carrying out chores, Cassidy dismounted and sat on a small rock.

'We're at the desert now. What do you reckon?' Cassidy asked once Nathaniel had joined him. 'Are we looking for outlaws or too much sand and sun?'

Nathaniel rummaged in his buckskin jacket-pocket and produced a sheet of paper.

'Never been in a desert before and I reckon it can kill a man who ain't careful, but I figure we're searching for one of these men.'

Cassidy grabbed the sheet of paper and ran his gaze down the short list of names.

Before leaving Beaver Ridge, he'd noted the details of outlaws who favoured attacking in bandit-style ambushes and had headed west. Top of the list was Frank Chapel, followed by his brother, Vince Chapel, Lex Thompson, Miles McGiven and Silas Fenshaw. These men were all vicious outlaws and intelligent enough to avoid capture. Not having met any of them, knowing their past didn't help Cassidy. Worse, these were just the known outlaws.

Cassidy pocketed the list.

'Maybe we are looking for one of these men. So we'll note their names before we arrest them and keep our records straight.'

As the sound of footsteps approached, Cassidy looked up.

Olivia Smith strode towards them brandishing a bucket.

Nathaniel shuffled backward on his rock.

'Here comes trouble,' he mumbled.

Cassidy forced a smile.

'Hello, Olivia. Are we ready to go?'

While tapping one booted foot on the ground, Olivia threw her long grey-streaked hair back from her hard-boned face.

Cassidy widened his smile. Olivia's green eyes flared.

To date, Cassidy had learned that Olivia had two moods: loud and irritable, or silent and annoyed. If this was the latter, self-preservation was in order.

Cassidy jumped to his feet. 'Do chores need doing?'

'You're right,' she screeched. 'You're fairly intelligent for a man.'

She threw the bucket down at his feet. Without further comment, she swirled round. Her skirts billowed in a wide circle as she stormed back to the wagon train.

'We escaped lightly,' Nathaniel said. 'I thought she'd lecture us again.'

Cassidy grabbed the bucket and pondered which of the dozen or so uses for a bucket Olivia wanted them to put it to.

'We escaped the lecture, but if you don't move from that rock, she'll bring out the broom.'

Smiling ruefully, Nathaniel leapt to his feet. They wandered back to the wagon train. On the way, Nathaniel nudged Cassidy in the ribs.

'Who do you think would come off best in a fight between Frank Chapel with his two guns and Olivia Smith with her broom?'

Cassidy smiled. Strangely, he wasn't sure of the answer.

THREE

In the middle of the baking afternoon, Cassidy approached a small collection of buildings. The rough adobe houses huddled amid a vista of white rocks and sun-blasted sand. In the distorting heat haze, the buildings shimmered as if they were a reflection in a rippling lake. Cassidy couldn't tell if the buildings were miles away or hundreds of yards away.

Why anyone would choose to live in such an inhospitable place Cassidy didn't know and he hoped he never understood.

'Hell's End,' Nathaniel whispered.

'You don't say.'

'No, I meant the name of the town is Hell's End.'

Despite the heat, Cassidy smiled.

'I know. It just don't seem an inviting sort of place.'

Riding in silence, Cassidy and Nathaniel cantered to the front of the wagon train. They arrived at a rough fence and a sign confirming this place was the appropriately named town.

By the fence, Cassidy waited for Graham Wainwright, the wagon train leader, to join them.

'Looks like we're here,' Cassidy said, pointing at the sign.

Graham ran a plump hand over his thinning hair and mopped his brow with a damp handkerchief.

'You're right at that. Are we stopping?'

'Yeah, Hell's End is the last town for two hundred miles.'

Cassidy took a deep breath to holler orders, but stopped as Burton Smith joined them. Gaunt and hulking, Burton was Olivia's husband and vied with her for possession of the least appealing personality in this wagon train.

Graham turned to Burton.

'We're stopping here,' he said.

'Suppose I agree,' Burton said.

Cassidy dragged his horse round and pointed to a wide, flat space outside Hell's End.

'Graham, pull up the wagon train there while Nathaniel and I see what's happening in town.'

Burton encouraged his horse between them as Graham nodded.

'You may be here to protect us,' Burton said, 'but that ain't a reason for us to run scared every time we meet new folk. We should go straight into town. I've never hid from any man and I ain't starting now.'

'This is just another frontier town,' Cassidy said with his hands spread wide. 'There's no need to hide.'

'Yeah, but I'm sick of this routine of waiting outside town until you say we can move in.'

'I'm being careful, for everyone's good.'

'If this place is dangerous, we shouldn't be here. With nothing to be scared of, why do you need to go on ahead?'

Cassidy sighed. 'To discover if this place is safe. Just let us do our job.'

'Like I say, I've never run from no one. We'll take the wagons straight into town with you.'

Cassidy ran a hand over his brow. They'd had this argument at every town that they'd stopped at. Cassidy hoped that before they reached California he'd work out how to resolve it.

'I'm happy for the lawmen to protect us,' Graham muttered. 'They know best.'

Burton swung round to Graham, ready to debate this minor issue until sunset.

Cassidy shrugged to Nathaniel. To avoid wasting time arguing in the hot afternoon, Cassidy didn't wait for Graham to decide which orders he'd follow. He encouraged his horse to a trot. With Nathaniel a few horse-lengths behind, he rode around the side of the fence and into Hell's End.

The word 'town' was an overstatement for the dozen or so nondescript buildings and dwelling houses that lined the one road. Aside from a saloon, a store and a stable, Cassidy saw few signs that this place functioned as a legitimate place to stop.

If the proud boast that this town supported forty-seven people was true, those people liked each other's close company.

Cassidy halted his horse in the middle of the road. He trotted round in a small circle, seeing if he'd missed anything else in the town. He hadn't.

He dismounted. With Nathaniel at his side, he sauntered to the unnamed saloon, threw open the swing-doors and walked inside. The doors creaked to a halt. The sound gave way to the flies that buzzed lazily.

Inside, light-coloured sand coated the rough furniture and floor.

Cassidy kept his gaze on the three dozing men sitting by the back wall. The men leaned back in their chairs with wide Stetsons pulled over their faces. A town like this couldn't receive that many visitors for these men not to notice their arrival. If the men pretended to sleep, Cassidy wanted to know why.

After thirty seconds of silence, the central man pushed his hat back with a finger, revealing weather-hardened features with deep wrinkles etched across a face spare of excess fat.

'Who might you be?' The man's flat tone indicated that he didn't care about the answer, although his eyes widened.

Cassidy assumed he'd seen the badge.

'Name's Cassidy Yates, and this here is Nathaniel McBain. We have a wagon train. Aside from us two, we have nineteen people looking for hospitality.'

The man sitting to the left chuckled beneath his hat.

The central man lifted his hat.

'Lance Ponting at your service, general store-keeper.' Lance yawned and stretched back further in his chair.

Cassidy sighed. 'The general storekeeper of a town like this should be jumping at the chance of extra custom.'

Lance yawned again, prolonging the action with an extravagant stretch.

'You'd have thought so, but you clearly ain't been through this part of the world before. Jumping wastes energy. You can be happy to see new people while moving slowly.'

In demonstration, Lance slowly pushed to his feet. With his shoulders hunched, he shuffled to Cassidy.

'Sorry to ruin your siesta,' Cassidy muttered.

'Me too. I'll get Gordon.'

'Who's Gordon?'

'Nearest we got to a town mayor. Town this size don't need one. But we have Gordon and he'll do.'

'Forty-seven people ain't such a small place.'

Lance stretched. 'Ain't had forty-seven people here for ten, maybe twenty years. We had sixteen at the last count. I've been meaning to change that sign. Perhaps I'll do it later today.'

Lance shuffled through the swing-doors. Once outside, he glanced to the sun and then wandered across the road to a building opposite.

'I bet you he won't change that sign later,' Nathaniel said.

'No bet there,' Cassidy said.

Someone chuckled.

Irritated, Cassidy swirled around. He strode across the room and batted the chuckling man's hat from his face.

Beneath the hat, the man smiled at him.

'Afternoon, Cassidy Yates. Would you like a drink in my saloon?'

Although Cassidy was tempted to refuse, a sudden

image of a foaming cool beer floated across his mind. Unbidden, he licked his lips.

'Beer would be fine.'

The barkeep chuckled. 'Good choice. I serve the coolest beer for two hundred miles.'

Thinking of a beer, Cassidy's irritation at the lethargy of this town receded. He cleared a small sand-drift from the counter and slumped on a barstool.

'Shouldn't we check out the rest of the town?' Nathaniel asked.

'We'll check out the beer first. We need to ensure it's safe for the pioneers to drink.'

'Not known the pioneers to drink alcohol,' Nathaniel muttered. Then he smiled. 'But it's the best idea I've heard.'

Glass clinked. Cassidy turned as the barkeep approached holding two brimming glasses. The beers were the flattest he'd ever seen. Even that didn't annoy him. He grabbed a glass from the barkeep and savoured his first gulp.

Spluttering and swallowing at the same time, Cassidy slammed the glass on the counter.

'What in tarnation is this?'

The barkeep scratched his head.

'Beer, like you asked for.'

'I've had colder fresh coffee. You said this was the coolest beer for two hundred miles.'

The barkeep chuckled and made a small note on a slate behind the counter.

'Don't leave town without settling your account.'

Despite the warmth of the beer, Cassidy was thirsty,

so he drank half of his beer. The fusty taste nearly made him gag.

Nathaniel knocked back his entire glassful in a prolonged gulping swallow. With the back of his hand, he wiped his mouth and smacked his lips.

'This ain't that bad. I could get used to it.'

'Let's hope we don't get a chance.'

Someone hollered and Cassidy glanced outside.

Burton Smith had won his argument as to where the wagons should stop.

The wagon train pulled up by the stable and Burton spoke to a bearded man who gestured into the stable.

In the heat, Cassidy couldn't muster enough energy to be annoyed. He downed the rest of his drink and sauntered to the door. While leaning against the doorframe, he listened as Burton Smith talked with a new man. The new man was as lean as Lance was, with an aquiline nose that accentuated his spare features.

'What do you want to do?' the man asked.

Burton shrugged and glanced toward Cassidy.

'Got nothing to do with me,' Burton said. 'That's a matter for the law.'

'You sure?'

'I'm only part of this wagon train, nothing more.' Burton glanced at Cassidy again and then lowered his voice. 'If'n we were on our own we'd sort this. We ain't. See the lawman and let him deal with it.'

To himself, Cassidy smiled. He hadn't thought Burton would ever admit he wasn't in charge of everything.

The man wandered from Burton Smith to the saloon.

'You wanted to see me, Sheriff Cassidy Yates,' the man said in a languid drawl.

'You'll be Gordon?' Cassidy asked.

The man glared back.

Cassidy hung his head. Time spent with people who didn't waste energy on surplus movement or conversation would be tough.

When the man didn't reply, Cassidy nodded to the wagons.

'We'll be here until sunset,' he said. 'Then we head across the desert.'

'We call the desert Hell Creek.'

Cassidy pondered. With a creek in the desert the water would make the journey easier.

'There ain't a creek on the map.'

'We know,' Gordon muttered, stone-faced. 'That's why we call it hell.'

Behind Cassidy, the barkeep chuckled.

Cassidy smiled. Often in the roughest frontier towns where living was the harshest, the humour was equally harsh.

'Why call this town Hell's End then?' Cassidy asked, getting into the spirit of Gordon's conversation. 'Wouldn't Hell's Start be better?'

Gordon pouted. 'Depends which direction you're going. I suppose a sheriff is travelling with these pioneers because of the two missing wagon trains.'

With Gordon mentioning business, Cassidy nodded.

'Four are missing now.'

'My mistake. Out here, we don't get to know everything that happens.'

'Do you know anything that might help us?'

'Wondered when you might ask. We've imprisoned one of the outlaws who attacked the last wagon train. We're waiting for you to take him into custody.'

Gordon turned and sauntered across the road.

With a shrug, Cassidy strode after him, balking as the heat blasted down on his back. In his respite from the heat, he'd enjoyed the shade.

To his surprise, his enjoyment included the beer.

FOUR

Locked for three weeks in what was probably once a hotel room, the man should have been restless. But after his journey across Hell Creek, being shaded from the sun and having a regular water-supply was relaxing. Better, his blistered hands and face weren't as sore as when he'd arrived in Hell's End.

Conversation burbled outside his room. Although he was sure this wasn't dinnertime, he pushed from his chair and faced the door.

The door opened and two men he didn't recognize wandered in with Gordon. Gordon nodded to them.

'Got Sheriff Cassidy Yates and Deputy Nathaniel McBain here. They're ready to sort you out.'

The man held his hands wide.

'Afternoon, Sheriff. I'm glad to see you. I've wanted to see a lawman ever since I got to this town.'

The sheriff mopped his brow with a red bandanna. He tied it around his neck and folded his arms.

'Gordon tells me you were in Hell Creek close to

28

where Matt Travis's wagon train met its end.'

'Yeah.'

'And how are you feeling now?'

The man glanced down at his thin body and shrugged.

'I don't think I'm at my best right now. I spent a week in Hell Creek with little water and no food. But I ain't got much of an appetite since I got here so I'm still losing weight. Guessing as my Ma wouldn't recognize me now.'

'I'm sorry for you. What about the pioneers in Matt Travis's wagon train?'

'Everyone on the wagon train is dead. Somebody massacred them. Aside from that, I can't remember anything more.'

Gordon snorted. 'Mighty convenient.'

The sheriff glared at Gordon until he looked away.

'Tell me what you remember.'

'I just did. I reckon the sun burnt my memory away, so I can't be of use to you.'

Gordon hid his snorting response behind the back of his hand.

The sheriff ignored Gordon and stepped forward.

'I've never known too much sun to burn away your memory.'

The man ruefully ran his fingers over his scalp, considering. Since arriving in Hell's End, he'd discovered a number of sore spots he hadn't noticed when his life was in immediate danger.

'Yeah, but I think whoever attacked the wagon train roughed me up too. Someone might have hit me on the head.'

The sheriff nodded. 'That might do it. So, you don't even know your own name?'

The man shook his head. 'Can't bring one to mind.'

The sheriff rummaged in his pocket and produced two sheets of paper. He handed one to the man.

'Look at this list and see if any name is familiar.'

The man grabbed the paper. He ran his gaze down the eighteen names, starting with Matt Travis and ending at Willie Thornton.

'Sorry. None of these names is mine. I guess these are the names of the wagon train pioneers.'

'Seeing as how your memory has gone,' the sheriff said with his eyebrows raised, 'how would you know that?'

'Eighteen names are on this list. I counted eighteen dead people by the wagon train.'

The sheriff and his deputy nodded.

Gordon grinned.

The sheriff lifted his hat and ran a hand over his forehead.

'That's as near to a confession as you could make. Don't know whether it would convince a judge, but it's nearly convinced me.'

'What do you mean?'

'Matt Travis's wagon train started from Beaver Ridge. By the time it left New Hope Town, eighteen people were in the group. You just said that eighteen dead bodies are in Hell Creek.' The sheriff narrowed his eyes to thin slits. 'So who are you?'

With his head hung, the man ran a hand over the

back of his neck. For the last four weeks, this question had pounded back and forth in his mind. But he still didn't know his name or who he was before he'd spent a week in Hell Creek. The only possible answer was one he didn't like to think of.

'I know this looks like I was one of the outlaws that attacked the wagon train, but they left me to die in Hell Creek. I don't think I could be.'

Cassidy shook his head.

'I have bad news for you. I've dealt with plenty of outlaws and their type would double-cross their own ma if they could make a profit. Don't seem odd to me that they turned against you. Perhaps you wanted a bigger share of the pickings and they left you to die as punishment.'

Unable to meet the sheriff's hard gaze, the man considered the list of names. He mumbled each name as he willed one of them to sound familiar. None of them did.

The man handed back the list to the sheriff.

'Could be other explanations,' the man said, unwilling to stop hoping that he wasn't the sort of man he feared he was. 'The bodies at the wagon train had been dead for a while, but they'd fought back. It's possible that one of the bodies was an outlaw and the other seventeen were from the wagon train.'

Gordon laughed and stepped forward.

'No way, Mr Outlaw. I saw most of the pioneers in the last wagon train that passed through Hell's End.' Gordon grinned. 'I don't remember seeing you.'

The man hung his head.

'There could be another explanation.'

He waited in silence.

'You may be right,' the sheriff said. 'Don't sound probable to me. But until I can prove otherwise, we'll assume you ain't one of the outlaws.'

The man smiled. 'Thank you. I'll do anything to help.'

'Good. First up, we'll go to the wagon train. You'll show us the way.'

'What good will that do? Like I said, the pioneers are dead.'

'We can prove they're Matt Travis's group,' Cassidy snapped with his eyes narrowed. 'Whatever we find, we can give them a decent burial.'

The man hung his head at his unthinking comment. He'd blurted his response at the shocking thought of returning to Hell Creek. Explaining his comment now wouldn't help him.

The man glanced through his barred window. Beyond was the featureless desert.

'Reckon sunset is in four hours. We should go then.'

'We go now. I don't want to travel there in the dark. We need to see what happened at the wagon train. If needs be, we'll return in the dark.'

The man shook his head.

'The wagon train is some distance away. We might not get there before dark.'

The sheriff nodded. 'We go tomorrow at first light then.'

'We can do one more thing,' the man said as the sheriff turned away. 'If you don't mind.'

'And what's that?' the sheriff asked, while keeping

his back turned.

'Give me a name. Somehow, not having a name makes me feel like I don't exist.'

The sheriff turned back and shook his head.

'Not my job to give you a name. Pick a name. The first that springs to mind.'

From nowhere, a name entered the man's mind.

'Mattie,' he said.

The sheriff frowned. 'Mattie's a woman's name.'

'No, Matt. Matt Travis I suppose.'

As Gordon raised his eyebrows and the deputy shook his head the sheriff nodded and walked to the door. At the door, he stopped.

'Matt it is.'

FIVE

Once outside, Cassidy stopped in the centre of the road beside Gordon. The pioneers were now under cover in the stable.

He expected Gordon to complain about the decision he'd just made.

Gordon shrugged. 'Reckon you're making a mistake, but don't lose our prisoner.'

Cassidy stared down the road to the barren whiteness beyond the edge of town.

'Hell Creek is the most effective prison I've seen. Once we're out of here, Matt couldn't go far on his own. If he escapes, he'll either finish up in Hell's End again or dead.'

Nathaniel shook his head.

'Not true. Some people live in Hell Creek.'

'What do you mean?'

'If outlaws attacked Matt Travis's wagon train, they must be surviving. The first wagon train disappeared nearly a year ago and that means they've holed up for that time.'

Cassidy nodded, wondering why a gang of outlaws would choose to live in such an inhospitable place. He turned to Gordon.

'Is there anywhere in Hell Creek that somebody could survive for a year?'

'Not that I know of,' Gordon said.

'So, how are the outlaws surviving?'

'Perhaps they've happened across a spring.'

'Are there many in Hell Creek?'

'The founders of this here town built Hell's End around a spring. Having found one, I've never known anyone to search for another. Don't mean there ain't more. Just look for a patch of vegetation. There's sure to be water nearby.'

Cassidy imagined travelling for two hundred miles without hope of finding water. He shook his head and wondered again why the pioneers didn't take the more pleasant fifteen-hundred-mile southern detour around Hell Creek.

'A man needs more than water to live. Can't be much to eat in Hell Creek.'

'The occasional vulture flies by, so animals must live there, but the man you're calling Matt said the food and water wasn't on the wagon train. The outlaws stole that to survive. The provisions a wagon train carries should be enough to live on until the next wagon train comes through, and they attack it to survive.'

In Cassidy's experience, outlaws didn't kill for food to survive. Their motivation was greed. Even if they had a reason, such an excuse wouldn't stop him from tracking them down and arresting them.

'This here town is the only one on this side of Hell Creek, isn't it?'

'Sure. We're the one and only Hell's End.'

'So, anybody that travelled west into Hell Creek would pass through here, unless they had plenty of provisions.'

Gordon nodded. 'I know what you're saying. If outlaws came by, we should have seen them, but everyone who passes through here looks desperate. It's hard to judge between the legitimate traveller and the outlaw. Whoever passes through, we give them what they want and that's always the same: food, water, and the quickest route out of hell.'

Cassidy nodded and pulled out his list of known outlaws.

'Any of the names on this list sound familiar?'

Gordon took the list.

'No outlaw would be foolish enough to give his real name.'

'You'd be surprised. Most are proud of their name. They like to let everyone know who they are and what they've done. It's how they build a reputation. Look at the list.'

Gordon held up the list. The corner of his mouth twitched as he read the names.

As a good poker-player, Cassidy recognized the sign but said nothing.

With a shrug, Gordon handed back the list.

'Don't recognize any of these names.'

Cassidy debated whether to ask, but he hoped to leave Hell's End soon and never return.

'Which name did you recognize? I know one of

them is familiar to you.'

Gordon coughed nervously.

'Frank Chapel,' he said, lowering his voice. 'He came through here a year or so ago. He said he was starting up again in California. Couple of the towns-folk recognized him, but he was causing no trouble, so we let him pass through and wished him well for his journey across Hell Creek.'

'It's the duty of law-abiding citizens to stop known outlaws.'

Although Cassidy said the words in a serious voice, Gordon smiled back, and he matched the smile.

Gordon waved his arms in a circle.

'Out here, miles from the big cities, we don't have that luxury. We'll arrest the half-dead ones like Matt. Everybody else can go to where they're heading and we're glad to see them go.'

With Gordon mentioning Matt again, Cassidy asked the one thing that bemused him the most.

'What did you intend to do with Matt? You arrested him, but you couldn't hold him for ever.'

'I know, and that's why we're glad you happened by. You stopped us having to hang him.'

Frontier towns often practised vigilante justice, but Cassidy couldn't support it. Once, he'd nearly been on the receiving end of such swift justice.

'You couldn't do that.'

'I know. We ain't got trees around here, but I reckon you can hang a man from a big cactus.'

Cassidy didn't know if that passed for Hell's End humour, but he didn't wait to find out. He led his horse to the stable where the pioneers were getting comfortable away from the heat.

Olivia Smith swept the stable floor. As they strode to the horse-pens, she smiled with her lips as hard as the desert rock.

To give Olivia no opportunity to allocate chores, Cassidy grabbed a nearby bucket.

'What do you reckon she wants me to do?' Nathaniel mumbled.

Ignoring the question, Cassidy led his horse to a spare corner of the stable. From the corner of his eye, he saw Olivia advancing on Nathaniel, the broom held before her.

'I'm guessing that she's about to tell you,' Cassidy whispered.

SIX

Matt rose at first light.

Within minutes, Cassidy opened his door and led him from his prison of the last three weeks to the road outside.

Daybreak was one of the few times that bordered on enjoyable in these parts. The sky was a deep red with the brightest stars shining through.

The silence was almost physical.

Best of all, the coldness of the night slipped away as comforting warmth, carried on a light breeze, enveloped Hell's End. Before long that heat would intensify to a blood-boiling furnace, but for an hour or so, life was tolerable.

From the stable, Cassidy led an extra horse to him. With a short nod to Nathaniel, Matt leapt on to his animal.

Matt checked his allocated possessions. Cassidy hadn't allowed him a gun, but he hadn't expected that. More important was the water and he pondered whether the ten canteens were enough for himself and his horse.

'You know more about Hell Creek than we do,' Cassidy said. 'Have we enough water?'

'You can never have enough, but this should do.'

'It won't,' a strangely familiar, strident voice shouted.

Matt turned.

A woman stormed towards them from the stable. Her firm stride threw out her skirts as she walked. From ten yards away she glared at Cassidy, her long hands on hips.

Cassidy patted his nearest canteen.

'If we carry more water our horses will struggle with the weight and they'll need even more water. This amount will do.'

The woman widened her stance and breathed through her nostrils.

'Never leave a man to organize anything.' She dragged in a full breath and screamed, 'Burton, get out here.'

A hulking man led two horses from the stable. The man glanced at Matt, then his eyes darted away. He swivelled and fixed his gaze on the woman.

'I've got everything we need, Olivia.'

'Whoa!' Cassidy shouted. 'Burton, you ain't coming with us and neither is your woman.'

Olivia shook her head, sending the grey-streaked hair into wild spasms.

'And you'd be the leader of this here wagon train, would you?'

'Neither are you,' Cassidy whispered.

'Pardon?' Olivia screeched.

Matt winced.

Cassidy sighed as Burton leapt on to his horse and pulled alongside him. Cassidy pointed back to the stable.

'We're investigating what happened to Matt Travis's wagon train. This won't be nice for ordinary folk. You should return to the stable and wait for us to return.'

Olivia grabbed her horse. For the barest second she glanced at Matt. Then with a dainty leap, she swung into her saddle.

'Burton and me ain't afraid of what we might see. This affects us as much as anyone and besides, I don't reckon any of you have enough religion in your hearts to give a proper burial.'

Cassidy opened his mouth as if to say something. Then with a shrug, he swung his horse around and headed from Hell's End.

Matt followed, but kept a few yards back, wondering why he knew this woman and perhaps her man too. And more important, he wondered why these people hadn't mentioned that they recognized him.

Two hours from Hell's End, Matt recognized his first landmark from his journey out of Hell Creek. A formation of rocks shaped like a lizard with a long tail sprawled beside him. He sighed.

When he'd walked in the other direction, he'd travelled at night and hadn't searched for interesting rock formations. Now, knowing their location, the distance he'd walked surprised him. Although he couldn't remember if he'd walked for three days or four, he assumed that he'd covered a vast distance. Yet in two hours, his horse's steady gait had almost reached the wagon train.

Matt trotted ahead to draw his horse alongside Cassidy.

'The wagon train is in a gully after the next set of rocks.'

Cassidy nodded back at Burton and Olivia Smith, who rode a few yards behind.

'Reckon we should ask them to stay back and let us investigate?'

'Nope,' Matt said with a smile. Then he remembered his recognition of Olivia and Burton. 'Who are they? Do they run this wagon train?'

'After a day with them, you'd think so. Graham Wainwright is in charge, but these two butt in and organize everything.'

'Yeah, many pioneers are like them.'

Cassidy lowered his voice and leaned to his side.

'As I'm a betting man, would you like to bet on which couple in the wagon train makes the best of their opportunities once they get to California?'

Matt shook his head. He bit back the small joke he was about to offer and pointed at the scrap of white cloth swaying in the breeze a short distance ahead.

Cassidy stood in his saddle and nodded.

Before, Matt had hoped he'd never see what he'd witnessed here again. Now, he was eager. Perhaps soon he'd find the answers he needed.

The wagon train was much as Matt remembered it. The forlorn broken circle battled against an unavoidable fate.

The only element that differed from Matt's memories was the sand, which had built small dunes down the sides of the wagons, and the bodies, which were bleached bones now.

Without comment, they dismounted and circled in toward the wagons. They raised their arms, shielding their faces from the wind that funnelled through the gully and whipped sand around them in small eddies.

For a few seconds, they stood in a line and bowed their heads beneath the baking sun. Then Cassidy turned and faced them.

'We need to look for clues as to who the outlaws were,' he said, his voice low. 'We also need to check that the bodies are Matt Travis's group.'

Olivia coughed.

'Burton and I will check the bodies,' she said, her voice croaking. 'You use your lawman skills to worry about the outlaws.'

Cassidy narrowed his eyes.

Despite the situation, Matt bit his bottom lip to suppress a smile. This lawman was used to giving orders, yet he'd met someone who had no authority over him, but told him what to do.

With a small smile, Cassidy nodded.

'You collect personal effects and we'll check them out before we organize burials.'

Burton and Olivia turned to the wagon train and edged to the first body.

Cassidy strode to Matt.

'What should I do?' Matt asked.

Cassidy waved his arm in a circle signifying the wagon train and the gully.

'Now you've returned, do you recall anything more?'

Matt stared at the massacred bodies. To avoid saying that he remembered nothing yet again, he examined the surrounding rocks. He pointed to the highest boulder, towering hundreds of feet above them.

'This place is the perfect location for an ambush. A wagon train has to travel slowly to avoid all the rocks. With dozens of places for outlaws to hide, they'd pick off the pioneers as they pleased without fear of the pioneers shooting them.'

Cassidy nodded as he followed Matt's gaze across the rocks. Cassidy patted Nathaniel on the shoulder.

'Climb up the gully, Nathaniel. See if you can find any clues as to who did this.'

Nathaniel nodded and climbed over a tumble of boulders.

As Matt cast his gaze along the gully, he could see many places to hide. A proper search would take all day.

'Should I join him?'

'No, I'll search the other side of the gully. You can scout around and see if anything recalls a memory.'

As Cassidy walked around the wagons, Matt placed his hands on his hips. He smiled at the way the sheriff spoke. Cassidy seemed to view his role in this massacre impartially. Over the last three weeks, Gordon was the only person Matt had spoken to, and Gordon thought Matt was an outlaw.

The sheriff's trust cheered Matt. He wandered to the first wagon. There, he leaned against the burnt wooden base while Olivia rummaged through the clothing of one body.

She dropped a few papers on to the ground beside her. Afterwards she trudged away with her head bowed to examine the next body.

A few yards away, Burton was doing the same. Every time he found personal effects lodged in clothing, he threw them on to a central pile.

Matt wondered if he should help Burton with this gruesome task.

Then, with a quick gesture, Burton took something from one of the body's jacket pockets and shoved the object into his own pocket.

At first, Matt assumed Burton would then transfer the object to the central pile of possessions, but he slipped a letter into his jacket pocket too. With his steady, hulking gait, Burton then wandered to another body.

'Whoa!' Matt shouted and pushed from the wagon. He dashed around the side of the wagon to stand before Burton. 'What did you just do?'

'Nothing that your sort would understand,' Burton muttered without looking up.

Matt bit his bottom lip and waited until Cassidy clambered from the boulder he was climbing. When the sheriff joined them in the middle of the wagons, Matt pointed at Burton.

'I saw Burton steal from that body,' Matt shouted.

Cassidy raised his eyebrows.

'Matt, this job is terrible enough without saying such things.'

Olivia snorted. 'What would you expect from a murderer like him? Don't see why we brought him along, anyhow. We found this place without any help from him. We just followed the main westward trail.'

While shaking his head, Matt held on to the one thing he knew.

'That's as maybe, but Burton stole from that body. Check his pockets, Cassidy, if you don't believe me.'

As Cassidy turned, Burton reached into his pocket and pulled out a watch and a letter.

'I assume Matt means these?'

Cassidy sighed. 'You should put those personal belongings with the rest. No reason for you to take them.'

'Despite what Matt thinks, I'm no ghoul.' Burton glanced at Olivia. 'I'm sorry Olivia, but these items belong to Tom Tinbrush.'

Olivia shrieked and turned her back on them.

Matt remembered Tom's name from the list of Matt Travis's pioneers.

'So what?' Matt shouted. 'Don't mean you can take his belongings.'

'Tom Tinbrush is an old friend of mine,' Burton muttered while tapping the letter against his other palm. 'I intend to write to Tom's family. I'll tell them what happened here and return this heirloom. It's the least I can do.'

'Sorry,' Matt muttered.

Even with the sun bearing down on him, a flush of embarrassment heated Matt's neck and cheeks.

Olivia snuffled and rubbed her face. With her hand trembling, she pointed at him.

'Sorry ain't good enough,' she shouted. 'Get out of my sight! Tom and Sarah Tinbrush are old friends of ours. You can't claim my man would defile Tom's memory. What you did here is an abomination.'

Matt hung his head, feeling as guilty as Olivia thought he was.

Cassidy strode between them. He took Matt by the arm and led him from the ruins of the wagon train.

'Just when I was beginning to believe you had nothing to do with this massacre,' Cassidy muttered, once he was outside the circle, 'you say something stupid like that.'

Matt turned from the sheriff's accusing gaze. Looking up, he recognized a collection of huge sentinel rocks looming above him. He pointed at them.

'I'll prove to you that I had nothing to do with what happened to these pioneers. Come with me.'

With Matt taking the lead, they strode by the rocks and scrambled up a short incline. They crested the side of the gully and paused for a moment.

They faced the bones of three bodies, which lay splayed on the ground: a fate someone had planned for him.

Without comment, Cassidy went to the staked bodies and rummaged through their scraps of clothing. Job complete, he stood, shaking his head.

'Ain't any clues as to who they are.'

Matt beckoned Cassidy past the bodies. On the other side of a boulder was the location of his oldest clear memory. He had lain ten paces from the boulder, but once he'd paced that out, the parched ground beneath him showed no sign of the days he'd spent there.

He sat on his haunches. In the rocky ground were

several holes, which probably marked where the stakes had held him. Sand filled them now, making them look like natural holes in the ground.

Standing above him, Cassidy sighed.

'Sorry. Ain't anything here that proves who you are.'

Dismissing what had nearly been his open grave, Matt stood and turned round.

Olivia Smith stood beside the boulder, with a rifle held against her hip. She pointed with the rifle back down the incline to the wagons.

'Burton and I have checked all the bodies. We need to review what we've found.'

Cassidy nodded and walked by her.

As Matt reached her, he stopped and cleared his throat.

'I'm sorry,' he muttered.

Olivia snorted. She waved her rifle at the staked bodies and back across the gully.

'For what are you apologizing? The massacre, accusing my man, again, or for everything you did in your worthless life?'

Matt was about to give an honest answer, when he caught the implication in her question.

'The first time I saw you, I reckoned we knew each other,' he whispered. 'So, how do you know me?'

With her eyes wide, Olivia shrugged.

'Would it help you if I said I knew the man you once were?' Olivia muttered in a voice sounding older than her years. 'Would you like to know what a low-life you are?'

Matt knew the answer to this question.

'Yes,' he whispered, keeping the pleading out of his voice. 'Anything would be better than this hole in my mind.'

Olivia nodded and turned the rifle to point at him. 'I wouldn't be so sure of that,' she said.

SEVEN

Cassidy slid down the incline and joined Burton back in the centre of the ruined wagon train.

In the rocks above him, Nathaniel roamed from boulder to boulder, but as he hadn't called to them, Cassidy assumed his deputy hadn't discovered anything yet.

Although Olivia and Matt hadn't followed him, this didn't worry Cassidy. The heat was too great to get concerned about anything and with luck they were settling their differences.

In the centre of the wagons, Burton knelt beside a pile of possessions. A smaller collection of letters and personal items lay close by.

Cassidy pointed at the smaller pile.

'What have you found?'

Burton grabbed one of the letters.

'Plenty of letters. Do you have the list of people who were in Matt Travis's wagon train?'

Cassidy pulled the list from his pocket.

Burton took the list, bent, and with periodic glances

at the letters, he wrote on the paper with a small piece of charcoal. He sighed.

'I can't account for everyone on the list. I thought Matt, or whatever his name is, said eighteen bodies were here.'

'You haven't seen them all,' Cassidy said and pointed up the gully. 'Three bodies are beyond those large rocks, but they have no identification on them.'

Burton nodded. 'In that case, we're missing four people: Matt Travis, Rick Thorpe, Roger McGovern and Sarah Tinbrush.'

'If Matt is right, we should have found eighteen bodies. We must have missed one. Only three bodies are up there.'

Burton shook his head.

'No, one of the bodies belongs to a man called Walter Filey and he ain't on the list. His body was outside the wagon circle, so he was the only outlaw that Matt Travis's pioneers killed.'

Cassidy scratched his head. The sweat poured from his scalp beneath his hat.

'That doesn't follow. We can't make assumptions like that.'

'You're right, but the body has plenty of broken bones, so he probably fell off one of the rocks above us and rolled down here.'

Cassidy considered this information. The staked bodies from further up the gully were large and probably male, so they were Matt Travis, Rick Thorpe, and Roger McGovern. This left Sarah Tinbrush unaccounted for.

Cassidy gulped. Having expected to find everyone

dead, he should be pleased that someone was still alive. But if the outlaws had held Sarah Tinbrush hostage for over four weeks, a part of him hoped she was dead.

Trying to turn from such terrible notions another worrying thought occurred to Cassidy.

'If we've accounted for all of Matt Travis's pioneers except for Sarah Tinbrush, who is the man we're calling Matt?'

They glanced over their shoulders up the small incline.

A scream echoed down the gully, followed by a resounding gunshot. Cassidy fell to one knee. He dragged his Colt from its holster and searched the gully for the outlaws who must have returned. He saw Nathaniel, kneeling near the top of the gully, but his deputy shrugged.

Then another gunshot echoed. Cassidy recognized the sound as a rifle shot.

'Sarah,' Burton mumbled.

Cassidy glared at Burton and then thoughts of the missing woman blasted from his mind. The rifle shots came from further up the incline, where he'd left Olivia and Matt.

Cassidy leapt to his feet and dashed to the incline. Burton was just behind him. He rounded the large rocks and scrabbled up the gully, his pounding feet sending small avalanches of pebbles back down into the gully. On hands and feet, he crested the top of the incline. Bent double, Cassidy dashed past the staked bodies. When he reached the final boulder, Cassidy paused.

When Burton reached Cassidy's side he nodded to

Burton. They dashed from the boulder, guns drawn and ready.

The only person there was Olivia Smith. She lay on her back, holding her chest as blood pooled around her.

Burton cried out. He dashed to Olivia and knelt, lifting her lolling head to his chest.

Cassidy ignored them. He'd seen all the blood. She'd no hope. He ran his gaze along the rocks, searching for a sign of Matt.

Gunfire sounded.

Cassidy dashed from Burton and the dying Olivia. He bolted past the boulder. As soon as he reached the edge of the incline, he stared down.

Below him was Matt's thin form, running along the gully and heading towards their horses.

With Matt having hundreds of yards' start on him, Cassidy shortened the gap. At full speed, he hurtled down the incline. Caring nothing for where his feet landed, he slid down the gully-side, riding a wave of sand and rocks.

Near the gully-bottom he dug his heels in and fell backwards, to skid to a halt in a rising cloud of sand. He resisted his need to cough, steadied, and took careful aim over one arm, firing his Colt twice. The gunshots thundered as they echoed down the gully, but from a range of around a hundred yards, neither shot slowed Matt.

Without pausing, Matt leapt on to his horse. He trotted in a small circle and leant down, grabbing the reins of the other horses.

'No!' Cassidy shouted.

He bolted down the remaining incline, skidding on the rough surface. Once at the bottom, he hurtled to the wagons.

From ahead, two gunshots sounded as Nathaniel fired down at Matt.

Cassidy rounded the wagons.

In fright at Nathaniel's gunfire, two horses had trotted from Matt, but he had the reins of the other two horses in his grip and he led them at a gallop from the gully.

With his target receding, Cassidy fired his Colt until it was empty, but the shots were wild. By the fourth shot, Matt had disappeared into the shimmering distance.

Cassidy threw his hat to the ground.

Nathaniel's lumbering footsteps sounded as he dashed down through the boulders. He slid to a halt.

With a short oath, Cassidy spat on the ground.

'Looks like I judged Matt all wrong.'

'You gave him a chance to prove who he is,' Nathaniel muttered while rubbing his hand over his sweating brow. 'And it looks like he did just that.'

'He sure did. A pity that Olivia died to prove his identity.'

After forty minutes of hot work, Cassidy and Nathaniel rounded up the two stray horses. They returned to the wagon train to find Burton pulling rocks into a small burial-mound.

Although they said nothing, Cassidy Yates and Nathaniel waited while he finished the task on his own. They owed him that much. Neither of them saw

much point in burying the other pioneers. Their
bones would soon disappear beneath the sand, but
they didn't deny Burton his chance to bury the newly
dead.

When Burton had finished, they stood back with
their hats held low as Burton leaned over the rock
pile. Burton muttered a few words, then he turned to
them, his jaw set firm and his eyes wild.

'I know you think Olivia had a harsh tongue and
she did, but she was tough enough to forge a life for
herself when we arrived in California.'

Cassidy wiped a layer of sweat from his forehead
and put his hat on his head.

'Yeah, we saw she was an admirable woman.'

Burton nodded. 'Matt has taken her from me and
it's time to get that scrawny devil. He ain't talking his
way out of what's coming.'

With time to think, Cassidy knew what he needed
to do next.

'Sorry. There's no point in chasing after Matt. He
has three men's water for himself, and we have two
men's water for the three of us. Worse, he has nearly
an hour on us.'

'Don't care what *you* are going to do. *I'm* going
after him.'

Burton swirled round and strode to his horse.

Although Burton had every right to do what he
must do, Cassidy wouldn't allow him to get himself
killed. Keeping a few paces back, he followed Burton.
When Burton was in his saddle, Cassidy grabbed the
horse's reins. He fixed Burton with his gaze.

'If you want to go, I won't stop you. Nathaniel and

me can get back to Hell's End on one horse, but we'll have more chance of getting Matt if we're organized. We should return to Hell's End, stock up on enough provisions, and come back to get him.'

'By then, he'll be miles away.'

Cassidy smiled and glanced around. The endless unforgiving scenery was dry and inhospitable in all directions.

'From what I've heard, I don't reckon Matt can escape from Hell Creek without passing through Hell's End. The route to the west is probably too far for one man on his own, even with three horse-loads of water, and the mountains to the north and the plains to the south are too treacherous. Either way, he'll stay in Hell Creek. He'll probably return to the outlaws who raided this wagon train, searching for his own answers. If we stick together, we should get him and the outlaws.'

Burton looked ahead and then his shoulders slumped.

'You're right,' he whispered. 'But when we find them, the outlaws may be yours, but Matt is mine.'

Cassidy nodded. In this, he'd give no argument. He released the reins.

While staring at the featureless desert, Burton sat firm.

Cassidy dashed to his horse.

Riding double Cassidy and Nathaniel joined Burton and cantered eastward along the trail to Hell's End.

When they reached the spot where Matt's trail veered into the hills to the north, away from their route back to Hell's End, Cassidy remembered the other task they had.

They'd confirmed the fate of Matt Travis's wagon train, but one pioneer, Sarah Tinbrush, was still missing.

EIGHT

Four hours after they'd left the ruined wagon train, Hell's End shimmered in the distance.

Cassidy nudged Nathaniel in the ribs and pointed.

'About time,' Nathaniel mumbled.

Yesterday, when they'd arrived at Hell's End, travelling west, Cassidy thought the town was the least inviting that he'd ever visited. Now, he viewed it as the most promising that he'd seen for a while.

He even looked forward to the warm beer.

As before, nobody emerged from the few buildings to see them as they trotted down the road. Cassidy welcomed the lack of attention. He didn't relish the prospect of explaining to Graham Wainwright that he'd lost a member of their group, before the wagon train had entered Hell Creek.

Outside the stable, Cassidy dismounted and led his horse inside.

Burton stopped and stared at the saloon. After a few moments, Gordon emerged and wandered across the road. They talked quietly and then with an angry shrug, Burton turned and stormed into the stable. As soon as he was through the stable doors, he grabbed another horse's reins. With a few deft movements, he transferred his saddle to the new horse.

While Burton finished strapping down the saddle, Cassidy spun round.

'Burton, you ain't going straight away.'

Burton finished preparing his new horse and hunched his shoulders.

'Like to see you stop me.'

Cassidy sighed. After what had happened to Olivia, he didn't want an argument. During their journey back to Hell's End, Burton had done plenty of thinking and all of it was probably dark. Burton would lash out at anyone that got in his way, lawman or no lawman, and Cassidy wouldn't blame him.

Holding his hands wide, Cassidy strode to Burton's side.

'Let us rest from the heat for a while.'

With his new horse ready, Burton grabbed four canteens and filled them from the horse-trough.

'Had all the rest I need. Matt's trail ain't getting warmer. Every minute I waste is another minute I'll have to spend tracking him, and another minute before I get to kill him.'

All this made sense to Cassidy. Normally he'd be the one who'd encourage urgency, but tracking an outlaw across the harsh terrain of Hell Creek didn't operate under the same rules as elsewhere. This needed thought, especially as an unknown number of other outlaws could be out there.

'We need to plan and perhaps organize a posse of our own.'

Burton snorted and paused from his canteen filling.

'You reckon these pioneers can form a posse?'

Cassidy turned. At the back of the stable, the pioneers sat in a small circle, sadly lacking organization without Olivia.

'No posse then,' Cassidy said, 'but you and I need to plan.'

'Correction, *we* ain't doing no planning. *I* am.'

Without further comment, Burton filled his canteens, secured them to his saddle, and filled another four.

Cassidy joined him at the horse-trough and filled his own canteens.

'Whatever you say, but I'm coming with you.'

Without looking up and with only the barest nod, Burton loomed closer to the brackish water.

'Don't expect me to wait for you and don't get in my way.'

Cassidy stayed silent until he'd filled his canteens. He chose another horse and transferred his own saddle.

Nathaniel joined him as Burton led his horse from the stable.

'So, we're going with him? You'd better give me a few minutes to prepare.'

'Looks that way, but only *I'm* going.'

Nathaniel grabbed Cassidy's shoulder.

'We don't know how many outlaws could be in Hell Creek. I'll come with you.'

Cassidy shrugged Nathaniel's hand away.

'Which is why *you'll* stay here. We don't know where the outlaws aim to attack this wagon train, or even if Burton and I will be successful. Whatever happens, we lawmen carry out our duties. You'll ensure these people get to California safely, like our mission says.'

Nathaniel kicked a stone on the ground.

'How long do you think you'll be?'

'We can only carry enough water for two days. If we don't find where the outlaws, and hopefully Sarah Tinbrush and Matt, are holed up, we'll be back before then. You'll stay in charge of the pioneers until we return.'

'Any other orders?'

'If we don't return in four days, report to Beaver Ridge. After that head on to California anyway using the long southern route, but don't look back. We won't be coming after you.'

Gulping, Nathaniel ran a hand over his brow and mumbled indistinctly under his breath.

Cassidy noticed the sign; he patted his deputy on the shoulder. 'That was an order, Deputy McBain. You ain't to come looking for us. If we don't return, you'll look after the pioneers.'

'Yeah,' Nathaniel muttered, avoiding his eye. 'Whatever you say, Cassidy. But I wish I were coming with you. Things could get tough.'

Cassidy knew this. He hated dividing their forces, but in this situation, he'd no choice. He led his horse from the stable and mounted it.

As Cassidy got comfortable, Graham Wainwright

trudged across towards the stable. Graham raised his eyebrows as he prepared to ask some questions.

To avoid the difficult answers, Cassidy set his gaze on the desert.

'Things will get tough around here soon.'

'What do I tell Graham?' Nathaniel asked.

Cassidy smiled. 'Consider this your first task, as you're in charge.'

Nathaniel laughed, the sound hollow, and patted Cassidy's horse on the rump with his hat.

'Thanks. Enjoy yourself.'

Cassidy looked over his shoulder as he trotted down the road. Nathaniel turned from the stable door. With his hands on his hips, he waited for Graham.

NINE

From a rocky outcrop, Matt faced northward to the barren hills ahead. A few miles back, close to the trail to Hell's End, Matt had left two of the stolen horses. He hated to do this, but he hoped they might find their way to safety.

When Matt had run from the ruined wagon train, he'd had no definite plans. Two hours later, he was still undecided as to what he should do.

Although loaded with water-canteens, Matt now faced not only his uncertain past but an uncertain future too.

His encounter with Olivia was at the front of his mind, but however hard he pondered, the incident remained confusing.

For the third time in the last hour he removed the bandanna from around his neck and wrung the sodden cloth. From the little he'd learned about Hell Creek, he'd thousands of square miles in which to hide. More worryingly, he also had thousands of square miles in which to find death. His store of water and his horse only enabled him to delay the inevitable.

Matt clumped his horse to the highest point on the hill plateau and spun round, staring at the rocks and sand, which stretched to the horizon.

The only end to the unrelieved barrenness was the hazy mountain peaks that nestled on the northern horizon. Whether they would give respite from the heat and a route to amenable land, Matt didn't know, but if he travelled there, there'd be no second chance for him to go anywhere else.

Matt's only option was to head eastward and hope to get past Hell's End while avoiding meeting Sheriff Cassidy or Burton Smith. He swung his horse around and headed into the nearest gully, hoping to find an eastward route in what would be a long, unforgiving journey.

Once he was in the gully, he maintained a steady trudge along the rocky trail. He kept his head low to maximize the small amount of shade that his hat gave.

After a few miles, he received the first hint of how unforgiving his journey would be. From the hill plateau, the gully had appeared to run eastward around the next hill, but once Matt had circled the hill, the gully swung to the north.

He needed to lead his horse over the hill on his right and hope to find another route on the other side. Matt dismounted and picked a route upward through the sprawl of boulders.

He'd travelled fifty yards from the gully when, from the corner of his eye, he noticed a splash of colour moving across a landscape otherwise free of anything to catch his attention. Matt swung around.

Four riders edged toward him down the gully from the north.

He ducked behind the nearest large boulder. From there, he examined the barren landscape. Even if he hurried up the hill, they could head him off if they wanted to. Then he noted that the riders came from the north. They couldn't include either the lawmen or Burton Smith.

To meet the riders on his terms, Matt swung around. He led his horse as he picked a route down the slope toward the gully.

The riders spread out, filling the gully. They hunched forward and slowed to a halt thirty yards from Matt.

Once he was in the gully, Matt turned to face the riders and folded his arms.

Sand caked each rider's ragged clothing. With their heavy beards and hats pulled low, the men gave no sign of what they expected from Matt.

Even with the thick sweat coating his own body, Matt smelt their ripe odour.

With a steady hand, Matt tipped his hat.

'Howdy,' he hollered.

With a short oath, the man on the left flinched back, causing his horse to rear. When his horse was under control, he spoke to the next man. That man shook his head and narrowed his eyes.

The man on the left placed an arm over his brow, shielding his eyes from the sun.

With a short series of nods to the other men, this

man pushed forward. The steady clump of his horse's hoofs clattered on the stony ground. When ten yards from Matt, he dismounted.

'Afternoon,' the man said. 'What are you doing here?'

At this moment, the obvious thought came to Matt. Aside from the unusualness of meeting anyone in Hell Creek, these men were probably responsible for the fate that had befallen the wagon train. Such men would have no compunction about killing him.

His rifle was strapped to the other side of his horse, too far away to reach. This left him with his full gunbelt and the spare Colt Peacemaker that he'd taken from Cassidy's horse. Although since stealing the gun Matt hadn't fired it, the thought that he'd recognized the style of gun comforted him. With luck, in his former life, he was someone who'd used such a gun. Perhaps in the next few minutes he'd discover how well he used it.

Matt shrugged. 'Just passing through on my way to Hell's End.'

The man grinned. 'Why would you want to go there?'

'Heard it's a fine place.'

The three men on horseback chuckled at this comment. The nearer man shook his head.

'Hell's End used to be a fine place, but perhaps not recently. Things kind of changed there.'

From the little he'd seen of Hell's End, Matt didn't fancy arguing this point.

'Probably. But there ain't many other places to go to once you're in Hell Creek.'

'You're probably right at that.'

They waited in silence.

Matt didn't want to offer more, preferring to let the strangers reveal their intentions first.

Breaking the silence, the man shuffled forward a half-pace and released his horse's reins. The man looked at his hands and with deliberate slowness, cracked the knuckles of his right hand.

The man lifted his head to face Matt.

'Who might you be?' the man asked with his voice low.

This question had worried Matt, but no longer. Whatever the danger, he wouldn't lie. He'd lived without a name and he didn't fancy losing it again.

'I'm Matt Travis.'

The man frowned and cracked the knuckles of his left hand. 'Never heard that name, but you do look familiar.'

The man shuffled forward for another half-pace.

Unbidden, Matt backed away. Realizing this was the wrong thing to do, he stopped and stood straight.

'From where do you recognize me?'

The man strode a full pace and swaggered to a halt, five yards away. He scratched his beard.

'You're about thirty pounds lighter than your relation is. I'm guessing you're not another brother but a cousin. Am I right?'

Matt considered this question along with the answer to a question of his own. This man *was* part of the outlaw gang that had attacked the wagon train. He'd remembered Matt from that attack and, thinking him dead, he'd reached the wrong conclusion.

Giving himself every chance of leaving without violence, Matt shook his head.

'Nope, ain't got no cousin or other relation that I can remember.'

Matt smiled at his truthful comment.

The man stared at him. He rocked his head to one side and then twitched his right arm.

Matt ripped his gun from its holster, firing in a continuous movement. He shot the man through the neck. As the other men went for their guns, he fired in a line across them.

The gunshots echoed down the gully, repeating until the four crisp explosions faded to nothing. With the silence, the men lay on the ground, their crumpled bodies indistinct in a surrounding cloud of sand.

He'd taken each man with just one shot apiece.

The nearest man was flat on his back. Spreading blood coated the man's clothing.

Matt sighed. The man was dead.

In awe at the speed with which he'd dispatched them, Matt strode to the men who lay beside their horses. He'd hit each man either through the chest or through the neck.

He checked the state of each man. The first two were dead, but the man at the furthest right still breathed, although the swath of blood coating his grimed clothing said his life wouldn't continue much longer.

Keeping his gun trained on the man, Matt stepped before the sun. His shadow fell across the man's pain-racked face. Matt smiled.

'I was right,' the man whispered with one arm held over his bloodied chest. 'You ain't a relative. We left you for dead.'

Matt nodded. He didn't need confirmation that these men were his former attackers, but this truth cheered him.

'Your mistake.'

Without thinking, Matt put a bullet in the man's forehead.

The man gasped once.

Matt flexed his gun hand and frowned. When he'd seen that one man still lived, he'd hoped to discover more facts about his ordeal. Yet, as soon as he'd confirmed the man was one of the outlaws who had left him to die, his instincts had taken over.

Although Matt had learnt something just as valuable. He was quick to draw his gun and an accurate shot too. These were valuable skills that Matt was pleased he possessed. They'd be useful when he tracked the remaining outlaws who had attacked his wagon train.

With his future now certain, Matt smiled.

He stared at the dead outlaw and pushed the man's head to one side with the toe of his boot. Matt's smile widened.

He recognized the man.

TEN

After two hours' hard riding, Cassidy Yates and Burton Smith reached the spot where Matt's trail headed north.

Without comment, they veered northward and into the hills. With Matt, a missing woman, and a band of outlaws to find, the only action possible was to follow Matt's trail. Although Cassidy believed the man he sought wasn't Matt Travis, giving their quarry a name made the search easier. He wondered why this man had chosen to take the name Matt Travis and decided that desperate men would often say anything to get out of trouble.

They had travelled in silence so far, which was fine with Cassidy. Talking would dry his mouth more than necessary and create additional friction with his fellow rider. Burton had a mission and Cassidy had his own. With luck, those missions would coincide, but Cassidy knew where Burton's priorities lay.

Cassidy didn't fancy trying to persuade him otherwise.

For two further hours they headed along the trail that Matt's horses had left. Their shadows lengthened beside them as they climbed into the hills.

As the sun slipped below the horizon, they discovered the horses they'd ridden to Matt Travis's wagon train. The horses stood by the trail, sweating profusely, their heads hung in distress.

Cassidy glanced to his right.

Burton had his rifle drawn, clutched in his free hand.

The incessant heat had drained Cassidy. He didn't see that they had anything to fear from this discovery. He hunched forward and awaited developments.

They drew alongside the horses. The canteens, which had hung from the horses' saddles, were no longer there.

Cassidy hated cruelty to horses more than he hated cruelty to people, but in this situation, he had no options. He and Burton had enough water for themselves and their own horses, but no more. With luck, the horses might return to Hell's End overnight or they might find water, if any existed in this blasted landscape. If they didn't, within a few hours of daybreak tomorrow, they would be dead.

He urged his horse to trot by, avoiding looking at the distressed animals.

'Not right leaving them to die,' Burton muttered as they passed. 'Another crime Matt will pay for.'

Burton dropped his reins and lifted his rifle to his shoulder.

'No shooting,' Cassidy shouted, realizing what Burton was about to do.

With his rifle half-way to his shoulder, Burton shrugged.

'Why not?'

'We should give them a chance, and the sound of gunfire will carry for miles. It might tell Matt where we are.'

With the first grin that Cassidy had seen Burton produce, Burton swung the rifle to his shoulder. He fired twice, the horses collapsing.

'You're right,' Burton muttered. 'With luck, he'll come looking for us now.'

Although he didn't agree with either the sentiment or Burton's actions, Cassidy grunted an acknowledgement.

'Want to stop?'

'No,' Burton said, and then paused while he examined the darkening trail ahead. 'Except the trail will be harder to follow in the dark. Worse, we don't get much moonlight tonight.'

Cassidy pointed to a rocky overhang. They headed there and camped for the night.

Cassidy wrapped his blanket around his shoulders against the descending chill. Over the last few weeks, he'd spent many dull nights in the pioneers' company. Those nights would be preferable to the company he would suffer tonight.

He hoped they would find Matt tomorrow before the sullen silence that consumed Burton destroyed his own fragile confident mood.

ELEVEN

For an hour, Nathaniel sat by his horse on the stable floor, but spending time with the pioneers was only tolerable when he had Cassidy to talk with. On his own, he'd nothing in common with any of them. Worse, the group sat in subdued groups after discovering that Olivia was dead and Burton Smith was searching for her killer in Hell Creek.

Yawning, from boredom not tiredness, Nathaniel pushed to his feet and sauntered outside and down the only road in Hell's End.

With the sun having just dropped below the horizon, the temperature was merely warm. The desert was a variety of shades of red as night enveloped the land.

Nathaniel was happy enough to wander around outdoors now. In the heat of the day, time spent away from cover was a drain on your fortitude that you could do without suffering.

Within fifty yards, Nathaniel reached the edge of

town. He carried on his walk.

Three hundred yards from the road, Nathaniel came to a rough fence, which marked a circle around the town. He leaned back on the timber frame.

Within the perimeter fence were a number of rectangular areas, as if more houses had existed before, but no longer stood. The occasional pile of charred lumber hinted at the extent of this town when the population was at the level that its sign promised.

Nathaniel turned from this gloomy sight.

Thirty yards to his right was a small fenced-off area. With nothing else to look at, he sauntered to the enclosure. The area was a makeshift graveyard. Small mounds of boulders marked graves in several neat rows.

Nathaniel turned away. With his head bowed, he wandered back to Hell's End. When he'd travelled halfway back to the town he realized that the graves were identical and equally worn, as if the decimation of this town's population had occurred at the same time.

This thought further saddened Nathaniel. He wandered along the empty road and passed by the only store. He peered through the sandy window. Inside, rows of bulging bags lay piled to the ceiling. In such an outlying town, he'd not expected this variety and level of provisions. Although with demand being low, Nathaniel assumed that the provisions had probably been there for some time.

Having toured Hell's End, Nathaniel wandered down the road to the saloon.

Once he was inside the saloon, the barkeep waved. Nathaniel nodded back and sat on one of the stools by the counter.

The only people in the saloon were the same three people as yesterday, including the barkeep and the storekeeper. They sat in the same positions as if they were rooted there.

'One of your fine beers please, barkeep,' Nathaniel said, hoping that good cheer might lead to a more spirited evening than he'd suffer if he'd stayed in the stable.

'Coming right up. Although with the sun having set, the beer tends to cool a lot.'

Nathaniel took the offered brew and from his first sip, he didn't think it was much cooler than yesterday's drink. With a finger, Nathaniel made a small pattern in the sand on the counter.

'So, you get much custom around here?'

'What's it to you?' the barkeep muttered with a scowl.

Shrugging, Nathaniel gulped his warm beer.

'Nothing, just making conversation. Don't seem that a place this far out would get many visitors.'

'According to the sign, how many people live here?'

Not seeing what the barkeep meant, Nathaniel added a few more marks to his pattern on the counter.

'Forty-seven.'

'And how many live here?'

Nathaniel nodded. 'See what you mean, but you must get enough visitors to make a living or else nobody would be left here.'

'Just enough, just enough,' the barkeep said, and cleaned the sand from the counter. 'Let's hope you find these outlaws, or else nobody will pass through Hell's End again.'

The storekeeper joined Nathaniel by the counter. When the barkeep had finished cleaning the counter, he ordered a beer.

'I'd like to drink to that. Custom, and plenty of it.' Nathaniel lifted his glass to the storekeeper.

'I hope things work out for us.'

'Agreed. If more pioneers pass through, who knows how successful we can be. Maybe one day our sign will be right again.'

Nathaniel sipped his beer and turned to the storekeeper.

'May not be forty-seven people here, but where do the remaining townsfolk live? I've only seen you people.'

The storekeeper sipped a mouthful of his beer.

'The rest keep themselves to themselves.'

Nathaniel didn't allow the townsfolk's surly attitude to distract him, as it had distracted Cassidy yesterday. He smiled.

'Must be tough for you too. You can't get many chances to stock up on provisions.'

'True, but the air is so dry here, provisions stay fresh for a while.'

Nathaniel nodded, with some of the mysteries

he'd discovered in his short wander around the town solved. The other mysteries could wait until a natural point came for him to discuss them.

He settled down for the nearest to a pleasant evening he'd get in Hell's End.

As the first light edged over him, Nathaniel stretched. He yawned and slipped from his blanket. Although he was used to cold nights under the stars, here in the desert the night was as biting as winter anywhere else.

He'd spent the night outside to avoid sleeping in the stable with the pioneers. The accumulating smells of too many people in too small a space were bad enough, but on previous nights, the pioneers had sung too and Nathaniel wanted to avoid suffering that, whatever the cost.

As he stretched, people shouted in Hell's End. Bemused at hearing noise at daybreak, Nathaniel went into town. To his surprise, the five wagons were outside the stable, and as they were in a line, this meant only one thing.

Nathaniel dashed to the first wagon, where Graham Wainwright sat, his hands gripping the reins. He stood before the horses, arms wide.

'What do you think you're doing?'

'What does it look like?' Graham shouted back. His mouth curled in a sneer. 'We've had our rest in Hell's End and it's time to move on.'

'But Sheriff Cassidy is in Hell Creek tracking the outlaws who raided Matt Travis's wagon train. It ain't safe for you to travel yet.'

Graham shook the reins.

'We discussed this last night while you were avail-ing yourself of the foul brew in the saloon. We decided that Hell's End is as dangerous a location as any other around here is, so we might as well cross Hell Creek now.'

Nathaniel winced. This was correct thinking, but it opposed his instructions. At best, Cassidy wouldn't return for another day.

'But we should travel across the desert by night,' he said with his hands on his hips. 'Wait until sun-set.'

Graham glanced over his shoulder. In the line of wagons, the pioneers had either climbed into their wagons or were waiting on horseback.

'Sooner we set off, the sooner we arrive.' Graham turned back to Nathaniel and lifted the reins high. 'Stand aside and let us be on with our business.'

Nathaniel stood aside. If they wanted to go, he couldn't stop them, but he wouldn't let them leave without trying his utmost to change their minds.

'What about Burton Smith?' Nathaniel shouted, standing beside the lead horse. 'He's searching for Olivia's killer. You must wait for him.'

Graham shrugged. Graham's wife coughed.

'By rights,' Graham said, 'perhaps we should wait, but Burton and Olivia only joined the wagon train at New Hope Town. Worse, they didn't bring a wagon or add many provisions to the group. We don't owe Burton Smith any favours, but if he wants to catch us later, we'll make him welcome.'

Nathaniel wandered around Graham's lead horse

to stand looking up at him.

'How can Burton do that? Nobody can cross Hell Creek on their own.'

Graham shrugged, a small smile playing on his lips.

His wife coughed again.

Nathaniel nodded. He could see how Burton and Olivia's grating personalities had annoyed the pioneers, and had perhaps been especially annoying to the man who was supposed to be leading the group.

'I'm coming with you,' Nathaniel said with a sigh.

'Your decision,' Graham shouted.

He cracked his reins and the wagon lurched forward.

If this was his decision, Nathaniel wouldn't stay with them, but he was a lawman. He must help them, even if they didn't want his help.

'True, but promise me that at the first sign of danger, you'll hand over control without an argument.'

As Graham forced his horses into a steady trot, he hung round the side of his wagon.

'Protection is what you're here to do,' he shouted.

While shaking his head, Nathaniel hurried around the back of Graham's wagon. As he dashed to the stable, he wondered if he should worry more about Cassidy's reaction to his failure to ensure the pioneers followed orders or about the journey across Hell Creek.

By the time Nathaniel was on his horse, the sun had slipped above the horizon. With the first blast of heat, Nathaniel decided he had more to fear from Hell Creek.

TWELVE

Cassidy awoke at sunrise. With no food and no wood to make a fire with, he had concentrated on sleep during the night. His last sight before sleeping was Burton sitting staring from their camp at the horizon. He had half expected Burton to be gone when he awoke.

But Burton sat hunched over his rifle examining the rolling hills around them.

'Have you spent the night in the same position?' Cassidy asked.

Burton glanced back at him and then turned back to the hills. Unable to think of anything to say that would shake Burton's black mood, Cassidy tended to his horse. As soon as he was ready, he rode from the overhang.

Burton followed without a word.

They followed Matt's trail. The general direction was northward, but after an hour, Matt's trail spun round to go eastward. They edged down a steep slope into a gully.

When they reached the bottom, suddenly a gunshot rang out. Cassidy's horse reared. He got it under control and looked around, but he couldn't see where the shot came from. Around them, hundreds of convenient boulders lay, spreading up the slopes on either side of them. A man could hide behind any of the boulders.

Cassidy dismounted and dashed for the nearest boulder.

Burton followed and crashed down beside him.

'Matt,' he whispered.

Frowning, Cassidy concentrated on roving his gaze along the gully, searching for a hint of where the attack came from. A flash of reflected light or a puff of sand from a person scrabbling between boulders would help.

'We can't know for sure.'

Burton lay back against the boulder and ran a hand along his rifle, cleaning the sand away.

'No one else would be fool enough to be here.'

Cassidy nodded and hazarded a glance over the top of their boulder. Beyond, only a further expanse of rocks and boulders faced him. He ducked.

'Don't forget, the outlaw gang that attacked the wagon is here somewhere.'

'Maybe, but the outlaw gang ain't one man.'

'Can't know for sure that only one man is out there.'

With his rifle clean, Burton checked the barrel of his Peacemaker.

'True, but if more than one man was there, they'd have fired together and took us out before we responded.'

Cassidy liked this thinking. He'd missed having Nathaniel around to share ideas with. As Burton had started to be more companionable, Cassidy pointed further up the gully.

'I can get a better view of what we're facing from a different position. Cover me.'

Burton spun round to stare over the top of the boulder, his gun hand resting on the rock.

'Sure.'

Cassidy leapt over their boulder and snaked up the gully, keeping his head low. Gunshots sounded around him, but they came from behind. When he'd counted six shots, he leapt to the ground behind the nearest boulder.

He waited for retaliatory gunfire that didn't come and then lifted his head to search for signs of where their attacker was hiding. His new position only gave him a different view of the barren gully.

Cassidy lifted his hat to wipe his brow while he wondered what else to do. In a stand-off like this, the most patient man would win, but being patient in comfort was different from being patient trapped under the baking sun.

As Cassidy considered different tactics, from fifty yards up the slope a small funnel of sand billowed behind a boulder. He smiled. The sand could be innocent, but Cassidy didn't think so and he backed his hunches.

He stood and lowered his hat. With one foot raised on a rock, he rested his Colt over his arm. Keeping his gaze on the sand cloud, Cassidy waited for the attacker to emerge from behind the boulder.

He ignored the thought that he might be wrong and the attacker could be in another place. When he worked with Nathaniel, they worked as a team. Nathaniel would look out for him, covering the places Cassidy couldn't see.

He hoped Burton acted in the same manner.

After a minute during which Cassidy stood poised and ready to fire, a man shuffled around the side of the boulder he was watching. Cassidy wasted no time on pondering who the man might be. He fired twice.

The man clutched his chest on the second shot and fell on to his front. With terrible inevitable slowness, the man tumbled over a rock and fell twenty feet straight down to land out of sight.

Dismissing this man from his thoughts, Cassidy ducked to his haunches. If the man were alone, he'd have no fight left in him, but if he had an accomplice, the response would come now.

Someone shouted. Cassidy spun round to place his back to the covering boulder.

Burton charged toward him down the gully.

Cassidy waved his arms downward.

'Get behind cover,' he shouted. 'Others could still be out there.'

Burton charged straight for him.

With no choice other than to cover Burton, Cassidy leapt to his feet and fired four times in all directions. Then, with a practised dexterity, he reloaded. With one foot raised on the boulder, he examined the gully.

The only movement was the dispersing sand cloud near their would-be attacker. He accepted that their attacker was on his own.

Burton's frantic footsteps thundered behind Cassidy. He spun round and walked straight into a round-armed punch from Burton. The blow knocked Cassidy backwards for him to tumble over the boulder. Lying flat on his back, he shook his head.

Burton stormed around the boulder.

Cassidy rubbed his jaw. He was glad to find little pain, the blow being more glancing than damaging.

With his eyes wild, Burton kicked at the ground beside Cassidy's head.

'I never hit a man while he's down. Get up so I can knock you down again.'

Cassidy rubbed his jaw some more and then nodded.

'The man I shot wasn't the man we're calling Matt Travis. I don't know who he is, but he ain't the man you want.'

Burton slammed his foot on the ground, producing a cloud of sand and spun round, mumbling.

Cassidy pushed to his feet and batted the worst of the sand from his clothes.

'No need to mention it.'

'What?' Burton snapped with his back turned.

'You're supposed to say that you're sorry and I tell you not to mention it,' Cassidy said, although the attempt to lighten Burton's mood was probably not worth taking.

Burton spun round and spat on the ground before Cassidy's boots.

'No need. I ain't sorry. You need to know that if

you get between Matt and me I'll bust more than your jaw.'

Cassidy didn't press the point. Normally he'd not take kindly to anyone hitting him. In the circumstances, he gave a little leeway, but not much.

'You misunderstood and hit me once. That's fine, but hit me again, and I'll be the last person you hit.'

'Didn't think you'd be the sort to hide behind a badge.'

Cassidy tapped his badge. 'I'm not. I'm telling you that as a man, not as a lawman.'

Burton smiled briefly.

'All right,' he muttered.

With this being the likely extent of their mutual understanding, Cassidy lifted a hand.

'Wait here while I check our attacker.'

Cassidy edged around his covering boulder. Although he was sure no one else watched them, if the man he'd hit lived, he might try something. A badly hurt man could still kill you. Often, they had nothing else left to live for.

Doubled-up, Cassidy dashed to the nearest rock at the start of the slope. Beside the rock, he crouched. Up the slope, boulders were everywhere. The attacker could have fallen behind dozens of hiding places.

Cassidy craned his head, examining the general region where he thought the man had fallen. With precise care, Cassidy picked a route between the rocks and edged up the slope.

After a few yards, he found the fallen man. No ambush would come from him. The attacker lay on his back, his body bent at a sickening angle.

Cassidy gulped.

The man held a shaking arm over his head, shading his face from the merciless sun.

With no choice, if he was to gain information, Cassidy advanced a pace, his Colt held ready in case of a sudden attack.

The man twitched and gasped as he lay on the hard ground, his eyes more white than colour.

Cassidy stood above him.

'Hurt bad?' Cassidy whispered.

The man gasped with a small bubble of blood escaping from his blistered lips.

Cassidy knelt and gazed down at the crooked body. Although Cassidy had no doctoring skills, he judged that this man only had a short time, luckily. He dragged the dying man's gun from its holster, threw it aside, and then holstered his own Colt. He ensured that his shadow was over the fellow's face.

'How many more of your outlaw friends are here and where are they hiding?'

The man smiled weakly and then coughed.

'We have plenty of men, but I ain't helping you find them. They'll find you.'

Cassidy hadn't expected help, but he'd known men to give valuable information at the end. He needed to discover if this man would too.

'You may not want to tell me where you were hiding. But tell me your name and who you worked for. Every man deserves burial with a name over his grave.'

Although Cassidy didn't intend to waste time by burying this man, he hoped the request sounded genuine. Cassidy unhooked his canteen from his shoulder and dribbled water over the man's lips.

Despite his pain, the fellow gulped the water and then coughed. The coughing forced a deep wince from him.

'Name's Morton Fallow. I'm part of Vince Chapel's gang.'

Cassidy nodded. Vince Chapel was a name on his list of the possible outlaws who were to blame for what was happening in Hell Creek.

'How long you been surviving in Hell Creek?' Cassidy asked hoping to push Morton into boasting. 'This place must take some fortitude to live in.'

'Does at that,' the outlaw muttered through clenched teeth. 'We've been here about a year. I came with Frank Chapel. We joined his brother, Vince, and his men, but Frank and Vince argued over Frank's woman, Matilda. Vince snapped and killed Frank. Afterward, we joined under him. We're Vince Chapel's riders from hell now.'

Morton stopped his explanation to chuckle, the sound turning into prolonged coughing. When the coughing ended, Morton lay back, staring at the sky.

'When you raided the last wagon, you kidnapped a woman. Is she still alive?'

Cassidy didn't think Morton would respond, but he turned to him.

'What woman?' Morton whispered. 'We didn't take a woman.'

Burton walked towards them.

Cassidy stood and turned from the dying man. 'Burton, I told you to stay back,' he said.

'Won't succeed in tracking Matt if I stay away from danger. Anyhow, he don't look as if he can cause trouble. Has he seen Matt?'

'No, he's talked some, but he hasn't mentioned Matt.'

'Yeah, but from what I've just heard, you've only asked him about Frank and Vince Chapel. Mind if I question him?'

Having obtained as much information as he thought he'd receive, and more than he expected, Cassidy shrugged.

'Ask away.'

Burton sauntered past Cassidy.

'What do you want?' Morton whispered.

Cassidy left them. He decided to check the route Morton had taken into the gully.

A single gunshot rang out.

With his Colt drawn and ready, Cassidy swirled around and dropped to one knee.

An eddy of gunsmoke passed across Morton's body, Burton standing over him.

Cassidy dashed back to them. He grabbed Burton by the arm and spun him round.

Burton grinned, his smile gleaming in the early morning light.

Cassidy pointed at the dead man.

'Why did you do that?'

'Man was all broken. I did him a favour. Like with those horses.'

'You don't kill a defenceless man like that.'

'And you'd be the compassionate lawman would you? You'd let him die, crawling around on his belly for the rest of the day, I suppose?'

Although Burton was right in some ways, Cassidy was in charge of this expedition and Burton had shown no respect for that.

'Did he say anything?' Cassidy said, lowering his voice, although he wasn't backing down.

'Nope. Don't reckon he'd know where Matt is.'

'I knew that, but I wanted to know where the outlaws' hideout is.'

Burton shrugged. 'Seems that you and me want different things. I don't care about outlaws. I no longer care if they've abducted Sarah Tinbrush either.'

'I thought Sarah and Tom Tinbrush were supposed to be friends of yours?'

'Yeah, but they were friends in a former life,' Burton said, not meeting Cassidy's eyes. 'Either way, it don't seem to me that you care about tracking Matt.'

Cassidy sighed. Since yesterday afternoon, he'd expected this argument. Perhaps before they spent more time in each other's company, they needed to settle their differences.

'I do care about finding Matt,' Cassidy said, starting with something they could agree on. 'I can't see any way to excuse him killing Olivia and he should pay for his crime. You have the right to make him pay first. If you don't succeed, I promise you that I'll finish him.'

Burton holstered his gun.

'I suppose I should thank you for that promise, but that's only half of it. You're also in Hell Creek searching for Vince Chapel's riders from hell, and I'm not. Sooner or later, we'll end our allegiance.'

'Yeah,' Cassidy muttered, 'sooner or later.'

'My feelings exactly. Sooner it is.'

Burton stormed by Cassidy and down the slope.

Cassidy hadn't meant to dismiss Burton. He'd been trying to calm the confrontation. He followed Burton to try to keep them together for one last time.

'Burton, which way are you heading?' Cassidy asked from a few paces away.

'What's it to you?' Burton muttered without slowing his journey down the slope.

'We should stay together if we're heading in the same direction.'

At the bottom of the gully, Burton glanced at the sun.

'I'm going east to Hell's End.'

This surprised Cassidy. He dashed to Burton and spun him round.

'Why return to Hell's End? We can stay here for another day, maybe longer.'

With his shoulders hunched, Burton bunched his fists until the knuckles cracked.

'Matt's trail headed eastward. Seems to me he's realized that the only way to leave Hell Creek is through Hell's End, so I'm going there. If I pick the right route, I should get there first.'

With a hand on Burton's shoulder, Cassidy pointed along the gully.

'From what I can see, there are trails heading in all directions. You can't know for sure that any of them is Matt's trail.'

'You may be right, but soon, he'll head to Hell's End. When he does, I'll be waiting for him.'

'Even with an eastward trail from here, he might not head to Hell's End.'

'He will,' Burton said. He lowered his voice to a whisper. 'That's what I'd do.'

Burton shrugged from Cassidy's grip and strode down the gully to his horse.

Cassidy didn't stop him. He didn't need Burton's help. He'd worked on his own before Nathaniel had become his deputy and if necessary, he'd work on his own again.

He followed Burton, keeping a few paces back. At their horses, Cassidy mounted his own and without a backward glance, headed along the gully.

He rode a few hundred yards further north and found Morton's horse. Cassidy raided the provisions and then checked the few belongings for further clues as to where the outlaws might be hiding. As expected, he found none.

He examined the numerous other trails that criss-crossed the gully. A large number of people had passed this way and, more important, from the clearness of the hoof-marks they had passed by recently. Before he considered the direction of the trails, he glanced back down the gully.

Burton crested the hill to the east and stood framed against the endless blue sky. Without turning, he wandered down the other side of the hill.

'I hope you find what you're looking for,' Cassidy whispered.

For thirty minutes, Cassidy pondered the collection of trails that crossed the gully before he resolved them. Morton had been on his own and following several groups of riders who headed south and totalled around a dozen men. His more surprising discovery was four dead men lying close to Morton's horse. Fresh blood surrounded each man.

To Cassidy's way of thinking, this discovery meant that either the infighting within the outlaws was continuing, or Matt had encountered them. Cassidy liked the sound of the former thought better. If the latter were true, Burton would face a formidable opponent. But as Burton Smith had shown that he possessed a ruthless nature, the outcome of an encounter with Matt was unclear.

Having obtained all the information he was likely to find here, Cassidy pondered what to do next. If he believed Morton Fallow, Vince Chapel's riders from hell hadn't abducted Sarah Tinbrush. Unfortunately, they had accounted for all the bodies at Matt Travis's wagon train.

The only possible answer was a simple one.

Cassidy had assumed that the unnamed staked bodies by the wagon train were male, but he didn't know what Sarah wore or what her physique was like. She could be one of those bodies.

Cassidy nodded to himself. The abduction of one of the pioneers hadn't sounded plausible.

Cassidy mounted his horse and followed the trail southward. If he went north, he'd probably find Vince Chapel's hideout, but he was more interested in finding where the outlaws had headed.

After an hour of steady progress back towards the

desert plain, Cassidy's mind was free of tracking hoof-prints and considering plans. Then he realized that he'd seen Morton Fallow before.

The dead outlaw was the stable owner in Hell's End.

THIRTEEN

In the middle of the afternoon, Nathaniel encouraged his horse forward to ride alongside Graham Wainwright at the front of the wagon train. Ahead lay the lizardlike rock formation, meaning they were close to where Matt Travis's wagon train had met its end.

Riding beside Graham, Nathaniel pointed at the hills to the north.

'We need to head further south away from these hills and into the plains. That way we'll avoid taking Matt Travis's route.'

'Why?' Graham asked as he turned away.

Nathaniel had hoped they wouldn't waste time on this argument.

'Because the trail heads close to the hills and into a gully. There are plenty of opportunities for anyone to ambush us in such a place.'

Graham shrugged. 'Maybe, but I wouldn't like to get stuck in the plains. The sand might be thick enough to mire a wagon permanently.'

Nathaniel doubted the sand would be that thick. By staying on this trail, they faced bigger dangers from the outlaws. In his experience, these pioneers feared the dangers they didn't understand. They knew about outlaws but freeing their wagons from sand might not be so common.

Torn between which danger to avoid, Nathaniel decided.

'We should head into the plains. The sand can't be too thick. The risk from outlaws is greater.'

'Don't see that. Being away from the hills won't keep the outlaws away.'

'Yeah, but in the plains we can see them coming to us, instead of the outlaws seeing us heading to them.'

Nathaniel didn't add that either way, their chances of surviving were limited.

While frowning, Graham ran a sweating hand over the back of his neck.

'I don't know,' he said with his voice lower than before. 'What can we do with a warning?'

'If you can see what's coming, you have a chance,' Nathaniel said. He drew his horse in close to the wagon to make an offer that Graham couldn't turn down. 'Anyhow, perhaps we can meet halfway and head part-ways into the desert. We can avoid the hills, but not travel far enough into the plains to where the sand is too deep.'

Graham nodded.

With his first successful negotiation on this journey, Nathaniel pushed on ahead, directing his horse at a shallow angle to the hills.

Graham followed, leading the wagons off the trail.

Ruefully, Nathaniel smiled. From now on, he was in charge of what happened. To survive, they just needed luck.

After half an hour of steady travel from the trail, Nathaniel judged he was level with Matt Travis's ill-fated wagon train.

Nathaniel rode a hundred yards ahead of the wagon train. While he waited for the pioneers to catch him, he put his hand to his brow and surveyed the surrounding barren landscape. As he cast his gaze in a steady arc, a hint of cloth appeared to his left. He broke into a canter.

Within seconds, he confirmed that the cloth was the top of another wagon, which lay on its side.

As he cantered closer, further wagons appeared, also on their sides and burnt. The sand had formed dunes around the wagons. Within weeks, they would disappear into the sands for ever.

Sliding to a halt, Nathaniel examined the wagons, but saw no reason to dismount and investigate further. Three wagon trains had disappeared before Matt Travis's group. Whichever missing wagon train this one was, the bodies that must lie beneath the sand could stay there.

Nathaniel spun round.

Graham had veered the wagon train from their previous route and was heading to him.

Desperate to avoid this distraction, Nathaniel galloped back. He skidded to a halt beside Graham's wagon and pointed back along the route they were taking before.

'Don't stop! Keep on going along our route.'

Graham nodded over Nathaniel's shoulder.

'Is that another wagon train?'

Seeing no reason to hide the terrible truth from Graham, Nathaniel nodded.

'Afraid so.'

'Ain't you stopping to investigate?'

'Nope, everyone is long dead.'

With his head hung, Graham nodded.

'Shouldn't you prove this is the work of the same outlaws?'

'I've done that,' Nathaniel snapped. He didn't mind Cassidy lecturing him on what his job was, but this man couldn't. 'I'm more concerned with keeping you alive. So move on out.'

'Whoever did this is long gone.'

Nathaniel gritted his teeth at Graham's stating of the obvious and wasting time.

'It'll be night in a few hours. By nightfall, I want to get as far into Hell Creek as possible. If we do that, we should be safe.'

Graham gulped, as if Nathaniel's feigned optimism impressed on him the urgency they faced.

With a snap of the reins, Graham urged his wagon to move on.

A terrible thought came to Nathaniel. He'd headed into the plains to avoid the outlaws. But with the destruction of this wagon train in those plains, wherever they headed, the outlaws would find them.

Worse, the attacks occurred around this point.

With mounting dread, Nathaniel dashed on ahead to urge Graham to produce more speed.

FOURTEEN

Riding alone, Cassidy followed the gully southward.

When the gully opened on to the desert, the sun was high overhead and blasting down on him with its insistent heat.

The outlaws' trail continued to the base of the hills and towards the trail from Hell's End. Cassidy followed. From the distance of the horses' hoof-prints, the outlaws weren't riding fast, and from the inevitable remains the horses had left, they had come this way today.

Cassidy stared into the distance, hoping to catch a glimpse of blowing sand on the horizon as an early warning that he approached the riders. What he should do then, when faced with such superior numbers, was less clear.

In considering his plan, Cassidy's thoughts returned to Morton Fallow. Having discovered that the outlaw was the stable-owner at Hell's End, Cassidy pondered what the connection between the town and the outlaws would be.

Most of the town earned its living from the few

pioneers who passed through Hell Creek. For some, that wouldn't be enough. Morton Fallow would be such a man.

Running a stable wouldn't give Morton enough return to live on, so he'd sold out to Vince Chapel's riders from hell. Whenever a wagon train passed through, he'd warn them. Afterward, he'd return to Hell's End as if nothing had happened. Presumably, that was why he was travelling in Hell Creek that morning.

Morton had explained himself in other ways. He'd claimed he was originally part of Frank Chapel's gang, but when dealing with outlaws, Cassidy picked the small bits of truth from the wider collection of boasts and lies. In this case, Cassidy believed he'd found the truth and as such, he didn't like what he'd learnt.

Vince Chapel's riders from hell would be waiting in Hell Creek to ambush Graham Wainwright's wagon train. Whatever else he did, Cassidy would stop them.

When Cassidy reached the base of the hills, he found that the outlaw's trail had joined the Hell's End trail. He smiled. The outlaws had headed west and further into Hell Creek.

Although this surprised Cassidy, he didn't waste time on considering his good fortune. If the outlaws were heading west to set an ambush deep in Hell Creek, he'd go east and return to Hell's End.

While Vince Chapel and his riders from hell waited, he'd explain to Graham Wainwright what waited for the wagon train if they crossed Hell Creek. Graham wouldn't be foolish enough to risk the crossing and would have no choice but to take the lengthy detour. While the wagon train headed south, Cassidy would get word of his discoveries back to Beaver Ridge. With a proper posse, he and Nathaniel would flush out Vince Chapel's riders from hell without trouble. As a way out of the problem presented itself, Cassidy whistled as he trotted back to Hell's End.

Two miles later, his whistling died. He'd joined a collection of fresh wagon-tracks. He spun round. The tracks headed off the trail and into the desert plain. They headed away from where Vince Chapel's riders from hell would be waiting, but they were too close for comfort.

Cassidy urged his horse to a gallop and headed back westward. His heart thudded in horror at what he might find ahead.

For five miles, Cassidy galloped beside the wagons' trail and headed deeper into Hell Creek. He stared straight ahead. He'd pulled his hat low as he strained his eyes towards the sun, hoping to catch a glimpse of the wagon train before Vince Chapel's riders from hell found them.

Cassidy couldn't believe that Nathaniel hadn't followed his orders to keep the wagon train in Hell's End, but that was a matter for another day. He needed to reach the wagons, turn them round, and get them to safety before the ambush sprang. He didn't know if he could do that before nightfall, but he had to try.

As his horse slowed after such hard galloping,

Cassidy saw something. A faint cloud of sand was ahead, waving and indistinct in the heat-blasted landscape. Within another minute, the shimmering white cloth tops of the wagon train appeared.

He spurred his horse into a final burst of speed.

As Cassidy approached the wagons, a rider peeled from the wagon train and stood on the trail facing Cassidy. Although Cassidy recognized Nathaniel, he didn't slow his headlong gallop towards the wagon train. Every second Graham spent going in the wrong direction was another second that they would waste returning. Cassidy surged past Nathaniel.

Nathaniel dragged his horse around to gallop alongside Cassidy.

'Cassidy, you caught us,' Nathaniel shouted as he pulled level. 'Where's Burton Smith?'

Although Cassidy didn't want to waste breath explaining his actions, he leaned to his side.

'Burton Smith is back in Hell's End,' he shouted. 'Which is where you should be.'

'I'm sorry, but Graham wouldn't listen.'

Cassidy galloped his horse in an arc towards the lead wagon. In a huge explosion of sand, he skidded to a halt ten yards before the leading horses.

With no choice, Graham pulled back on the reins and dragged his horses to a halt mere feet before Cassidy.

The horses whinnied and bucked as they got comfortable with their closeness.

'We'll talk about whose fault it is that they came here later,' Cassidy shouted to Nathaniel. 'For now, we head back.'

Graham leapt to his feet, holding his reins.

'No chance of us doing that,' he shouted at Cassidy. 'Get out of my way!'

Dismissing Nathaniel from his discussions, Cassidy drew alongside the wagon. He stood tall in his saddle so that he was as close as possible to Graham's eye-line.

'You shouldn't have headed into Hell Creek.'

'That was our decision, so don't go blaming your deputy.'

Cassidy considered the empty miles of sand and rocks. Faced with this bleakness, impressing the urgency of their predicament on someone would be hard. But the wagons had halted, which meant he'd won half the battle. Now he had to win the other half.

'I ain't blaming Nathaniel, but I am blaming you, and your decision was wrong.'

Graham pouted. He threw his reins down and spread his feet wide.

'It wasn't wrong! I figured that Hell's End was as dangerous as anywhere else was.'

'And how did you reach that stupid decision?' Cassidy said, lowering his voice. Cassidy hated facing citizens who made decisions that lawmen should make.

'The decision wasn't stupid,' Graham muttered while waving an arm in a wide dismissive gesture at Cassidy. 'You were chasing Olivia's killer, chasing outlaws, and chasing some missing woman. I never felt safe in Hell's End. The people there seemed odd to me, so we left.'

Pausing before he gave Graham the bad news, Cassidy lifted his hat to mop his brow.

'Except I found the outlaws' trail. They're Vince Chapel's gang. They are as mean a bunch as you'll find anywhere. They call themselves Vince Chapel's riders from hell.' Cassidy grinned, as he let this pronouncement sink in.

Graham's shoulders slumped. 'We weren't to know that.'

'You weren't, but they're straight ahead, waiting for you.'

Graham gestured at the desert ahead.

'Could be worse. From what I heard in Hell's End, the outlaws could have been Frank Chapel's men. Everyone knows his men are the meanest you can meet. They say Frank Chapel even took on Marshal Devine.'

Nathaniel pulled his horse to stand a few yards from Cassidy. He shook his head.

'No,' Nathaniel said. 'They're right that Frank Chapel took on Marshal Devine, but the marshal ran Frank out of Beaver Ridge. Frank and his men barely escaped without holes in their worthless hides.'

Cassidy smiled at this comment. To press home his advantage, he edged his horse closer to Graham.

'After escaping from Marshal Devine, Frank Chapel came to Hell Creek. He joined his brother, but Vince finished what Marshal Devine started and killed him. Vince commands Frank's men now. The combination ain't boding well for anyone who meets such a group. You need to head back or you'll be dead within the hour.'

'Don't see no outlaws,' Graham muttered with his head hung.

As a good poker-player, Cassidy read men more from what they didn't say than what they said, and Graham was as easy to read as anyone was. Graham's decision was uncertain. Part of him wanted to return to Hell's End, but the stubbornness that was an essential part of all pioneers wanted to ignore common sense and push onward into Hell Creek.

Cassidy knew he'd learn in the next few seconds which way the man would go.

'Just because you can't see the outlaws,' Cassidy said, 'don't mean they ain't there.'

Graham lifted his head and stared over Cassidy's shoulder. While mopping the back of his neck, Graham sighed.

'We're going to California and it's quicker through Hell Creek. Now is as good a time as any to go. You'd better prepare to guard us.'

Cassidy knew that once Graham had decided, nothing he could say would change his mind. However vivid a picture he painted of the fate of Matt Travis's wagon train or the ruthlessness of Vince Chapel's riders from hell, the effort would be futile.

Cassidy nodded back down the wagon train and winked at Nathaniel. 'Suppose I ought to say good-bye then.'

'What?' Graham blustered.

Graham took a pace forward and nearly fell off the side of the wagon. He gripped the side.

'Yeah, I won't be guarding you, because I ain't coming with you.'

'You must protect us. You're the lawman assigned to look after us.'

Graham was right, but in the barren Hell Creek, the rule of law wasn't so clear cut. Cassidy hoped that Graham understood that.

'Wrong! I'm a lawman assigned to discover what happened to the previous wagon trains. Having done that, I need to report to Beaver Ridge.'

'Still means you must escort us to California.'

'No. Escorting you was a sideline. My main duty is to report where Vince Chapel's riders from hell are.'

The comment was weak. If Graham knew anything about lawmen, he'd know that no lawman's mission would involve abandoning innocent people.

'You're worth nothing as a lawman,' Graham muttered, scowling.

'True, especially as I'll report that I failed to keep you people alive.'

'We are alive. You can't abandon us.'

Cassidy forced a wide grin and prepared as big a bluff as he'd ever tried at the poker table.

'You won't tell anyone I abandoned you, because you'll be dead before Nathaniel and I reach Hell's End.'

'Don't worry, Graham,' Nathaniel said. 'We found that wagon train some miles back, so somebody might find your bones, one day.'

Cassidy nodded to his deputy.

'If they do, they won't know I left you to die.'

'You can't,' Graham whispered.

Graham's face was as pale as it could be in the heat of the afternoon.

'I can, and I am.'

Completing his bluff, Cassidy swung his horse

back alongside his deputy.

'Nathaniel, we have a mission to complete.'

Cassidy trotted back east, not so slowly that his subterfuge would be obvious, but slow enough to give Graham time to consider his decision.

At their sedate pace, Cassidy was alongside the third wagon when Graham slammed his fist on the wagon.

'Wait! You win. We'll follow, if you're failing in your duty.'

To press home his point, Cassidy rode for another few yards then pulled his horse to a stop. He swung round and leaned forward, nodding.

'We can wait and escort you back to Hell's End.'

Graham spat on the ground.

'I'll report what you said to your superiors,' he shouted. 'Doubt you'll like what I tell them.'

While smiling, Cassidy shrugged. He'd expected this response. Enough citizens had blustered that they'd report him over the years for that not to worry him.

'Maybe not, but you'll be alive to complain and that's all I care about. Now turn these wagons around. We have hard riding ahead to reach Hell's End intact.'

With much grumbling, Graham swung his wagon round in a short circle.

Cassidy glanced at the sun, which was halfway to the horizon. They wouldn't reach Hell's End before nightfall, even with hard riding. This didn't concern him. The biggest danger would come in the next hour. The further they travelled from Vince Chapel's riders from hell, the greater the chance that they would avoid an ambush.

As the wagon train trundled back east, Nathaniel drew close.

'Cassidy, would you have left him?'

No poker-player revealed whether he was bluffing or not. Cassidy shrugged.

'We'll never know.'

'Sorry I couldn't keep them from coming here.'

Cassidy didn't bear grudges for long. With the successful conclusion of this encounter, practical concerns had replaced his irritation with Nathaniel's failure.

'Yeah, Graham is pig-headed, but you must be more pig-headed than he is.'

With the wagon train heading back, Cassidy and Nathaniel led at a fast canter, riding fifty yards from Graham's lead wagon. With more men, Cassidy would have scouted around, ensuring he covered all approaches, but with just the two lawmen, he couldn't afford that luxury. More important was the need to push Graham to travel as fast as possible.

Graham's preferred sedate pace was no longer appropriate.

Nathaniel nodded over his shoulder at the wagon train.

'Perhaps we shouldn't travel so fast. The wagon train is kicking up a lot of sand. Vince is sure to see that from miles away. He'll know we're heading away from him.'

'True, but Vince probably knows where we are. I'd sooner return to Hell's End quicker and risk him spotting us.'

Nathaniel halted and turned round. He lifted his arm to his brow and stared back along their trail.

'Too late,' he whispered. Cassidy stared back too.

On the horizon, a funnel of swirling sand rose towards the sun, heralding the approach of Vince Chapel's riders from hell.

FIFTEEN

'Hurry,' Cassidy shouted at Graham.

The wagons hurtled headlong eastwards. The horses were at full pace, straining forward and sweating profusely.

The funnel of sand that followed them was closing fast. Within the sand were the outlines of riders.

'We'll never outrun them,' Nathaniel shouted. 'They can take us down as they please.'

Cassidy agreed. Unencumbered riders could match wagons with ease, but he hadn't given up hope that the outlaws might tire first. They had travelled further than the wagon train had travelled. And in the merciless heat of the afternoon, the toll on their horses would be terrible.

Cassidy clung on to this faint hope, but as the funnel of swirling sand expanded and the outlaws closed that hope receded.

Matt Travis's wagon train had proved that facing an ambush in a gully was the worst possible situation to defend. There, the number of places an assault could come from was endless.

In the open, the outlaws would need to take more risks and the protection of the wagons would benefit the pioneers.

With superior numbers of gunmen or superior skill, the pioneers ought to prevail.

Cassidy's charges had neither.

Cassidy searched the desert for any further advantage.

A small outcrop of rock jutted fifty feet from the desert ground a few hundred yards ahead. Making his decision, Cassidy pointed at the rock.

'We head for there.'

Nathaniel nodded. 'I'll tell Graham what to do.'

As Nathaniel swung back, Cassidy headed for the rock outcrop. Once there, he galloped around the rock and the flat patch of sand around it, familiarizing himself with the terrain for the battle to come.

With only five wagons, the protective circle would be flimsy, but with rock covering one part of the circle, they wouldn't worry about the attack coming from that direction. Better, as they defended less of the circle, they could move the wagons closer and get more cover.

The only problem this left Cassidy with was the one he could do little about: the fighting ability of the pioneers.

As the wagons approached, Cassidy dismounted and waved the wagons in to form a semicircle on the other side of the rock. On that side, he ensured that the attackers faced into the sun.

Although, to date, nothing the pioneers did had impressed Cassidy, they impressed him now.

On the first attempt they produced a perfect arc of wagons before the rock. Afterwards, they unhooked the horses and dragged them into the centre of the circle. Without orders from Cassidy or Nathaniel, Graham positioned the woman and children behind the wagons and placed the men between each wagon.

Graham waved for the pioneers to place wooden tables and other barriers between the wagons, and then trotted to Cassidy.

'Is there anything we missed doing?' Graham asked.

Despite the situation, Cassidy smiled.

'I suppose you've organized a defensive position adequately.'

Graham grinned with the widest smile Cassidy had seen from him.

'We ain't that useless. After the trouble with the previous wagons, we ensured that we could defend ourselves. Vince Chapel's riders from hell picked the wrong wagon train to attack.'

Cassidy couldn't stop a full smile from breaking out. But as he was unable fully to accept Graham's competency, he pointed at the rock.

'You missed putting someone by that rock to stop them climbing it and getting a good attacking position.'

'I'll get on to it.' Graham waved at one of his men.

The man dashed to the rock without asking what the wave meant.

With this display of efficient control, Cassidy patted Graham on the shoulder.

'Sorry I doubted you,' he said.

Graham nodded and marched away, barking orders.

Cassidy and Nathaniel dashed across their circle to stand next to the middle wagon. Cassidy looked back to the west.

The following outlaws were two hundred yards away.

With Graham's effective organization having bought them a few moments to consider, Cassidy turned to his deputy.

'What do you think our chances are?'

'If Graham's confidence ain't misguided, pretty good, I'd say.'

With a nod, Cassidy beckoned Nathaniel to position himself between the next two wagons. While he waited for the onslaught, Cassidy made his stance comfortable between the leading wagons.

Someone had laid a number of rifles between each of the wagons. Although with a rifle he might hit an attacker when further away, Cassidy didn't take one. He preferred his trusty Colt. His ever-present weapon had dragged him out of tough positions before and he trusted it to do the same here.

Shuffling footsteps sounded. He glanced back.

One of the children, he didn't know her name, ran between the wagons clutching a box of bullets. She laid a handful of bullets beside each defender and moved on.

In admiration, Cassidy shook his head again. He'd seen posses filled with lawmen who organized themselves worse than these people had, yet he'd spent the journey viewing them as without a hope of defending themselves.

He should have known that under-estimating people often proved fatal. He hoped that in this case, Vince Chapel's riders from hell would bear the cost.

Cassidy ran his bandanna over his sweating brow and tied it around his neck as he prepared for the forthcoming fight.

The riders from hell slowed to a canter as they swung round the rock to face the wagon circle. Fifty yards away, they halted and spread across the plain. They hunched forward in their saddles and sidled closer to each other. The group in the centre talked among themselves.

Cassidy couldn't see the men's features. Some had masks over their mouths and they all had their hats pulled low, but they were like Morton Fallow: dirty, unshaven, and suffering from the hard living of this unforgiving land.

Not having seen Vince Chapel before, Cassidy pondered which of the men was Vince. If he killed the leader, the rest might lose heart.

As he searched for who gave the orders, two riders peeled from the group and swung to the left. A further two riders swung to the right. Cassidy counted a further eight riders left in the middle.

If he discounted the women and children in the wagon train, the battle would be close to even. The riders were hardened outlaws, but men defending themselves and their kin could match such outlaws. Although in Cassidy's experience, they would prevail only if they were lucky too.

Cassidy never prayed, but he was prepared to pray for luck today.

With a whooping cry, the two riders on the left charged at the wagon train, followed by the riders on the right.

Cassidy knew this was a feint. They didn't expect to succeed.

'Don't panic!' Cassidy shouted. 'This ain't serious.'

He concentrated on the leading group who awaited developments.

The wagon train defenders fired a round of shots, all wild.

Half-way to the wagon train, the riders spun to the side and cantered back to the main group. The riders reported to the main group what they'd learned from their first sally.

Cassidy hoped they'd learned that this wagon train was better defended than the last ones were and so not worth attacking, but he doubted they'd be so lucky.

'Get ready,' Cassidy shouted. 'The next attack will be more serious.'

Getting comfortable, Cassidy shuffled behind his wooden table. Laid on its side, the table would protect him against occasional gunfire, but any prolonged barrage would take an inevitable toll on the wood. With luck, they could end this before that became a problem.

Across the plain, the dozen riders spread out. In a co-ordinated move, which in other circumstances would have impressed Cassidy, every other rider surged forward in a straight line and aimed for the centre of their defensive circle.

Cassidy only had time to note the riders hadn't made the usual mistake of circling the wagon train, giving the defenders the easiest chance of picking them off before the first horses reached the nearest wagon.

As a cannoning explosion of gunfire blasted into the wooden table, Cassidy Yates ducked. Splinters peppered his side as the wood kept the volley of bullets from ripping him to shreds. With a few moments' pause, a second volley blasted around him. Cassidy waited, knowing he must risk returning gunfire, but knowing that lifting his head would be fatal.

With a sudden lull in the gunfire, he darted his head up as a horse leapt over the wooden barrier.

Cassidy dropped to the ground to avoid the trailing hoofs. He spun on to his front.

The rider charged across the middle of the circle. Then, without firing a single shot at the pioneers, the rider, with contemptuous ease, leapt over the barrier between the rock and the first wagon.

Dismissing the rider from his thoughts, Cassidy rolled to his knees to look over his table.

The riders regrouped.

At a gallop, the rider who'd breached their defences joined the main group and the twelve riders backed as they formed into a line.

One of the pioneers whooped with joy.

'Looks like we saw them off,' the pioneer shouted.

Cassidy winced. The riders had designed that sortie to demonstrate to the pioneers that their situation was hopeless. The riders could breach their defences however they pleased. He kept these thoughts private. If the pioneers wanted to believe they had been successful, that optimism might keep them alive.

While they waited, Cassidy glanced at the man who'd shouted before.

The fellow mopped his brow. His eyes were wide. The hand holding his rifle shook.

The man knew how bad their situation was. He'd only commented to maintain everyone's spirits. Worse, Cassidy didn't know his name. After weeks spent with these people, the only name he knew was Graham's. Cassidy was thinking what to say to further improve their morale, when the riders spread further and hunched forward.

Cassidy crouched and gritted his teeth. The real battle would begin now.

Keeping low, Cassidy rested his Colt on the side of the table and waited for the riders' main attack.

The riders edged a few yards apart. Six of them peeled away and rode hard at the circle. As they charged forward, they held their heads low behind their horses' heads.

With the riders galloping and with little to aim at, Cassidy saved his bullets until they were closer.

As before, the riders fired a volley of gunshots, peppering across the wagon train, and the table Cassidy hid behind splintered.

Cassidy dropped to the ground. As soon as the

riders had ended the volley, he glanced over the table.

Six riders had stopped twenty yards away and spread out with rifles trained down at the circle. Behind, the second wave of riders galloped towards the circle, aiming to slip by the first wave.

Standing and facing this tactic was suicidal, so Cassidy knelt and aimed at the nearest rider. He fired once, the shot missing. Then a further explosion of gunfire ripped into the table forcing Cassidy to his belly again.

This volley lasted for twenty seconds. Cassidy feared that the table wouldn't deflect the gunfire for much longer. The bullets had dug great gouts from the wood.

A shadow passed over him.

He glanced up.

A horse leapt the table and afterwards a second horse followed.

Cassidy swung round to face the hooves of the second rider's rearing horse. For self-preservation, he leapt to the side, avoiding the flailing hoofs by inches. With his only option an undignified scrambling along the ground, Cassidy dashed a few yards from the horse; then, on crashing into a wagon wheel, he had nowhere else to go.

He jumped to his feet.

The rider fired down at someone lying prone on the other side of his horse.

Seizing his chance, Cassidy ran and leapt on to the horse, landing behind the rider. He looped his hands around the rider's neck and pulled him sideways. The rider flailed, but, sitting firmly in the saddle, he stayed on his horse.

The rider thrust his right elbow backwards, catching Cassidy a glancing blow in the ribs. Cassidy ignored the pain. With the rider off balance, he tightened his grip around the rider's neck and dragged him to the ground, falling on the man's back.

On the ground, the man gasped beneath him. Without pausing, Cassidy slipped his hands beneath the man's chin and pulled it back. A sickening crack sounded.

Only taking the time for a deep breath, Cassidy leapt to his feet to face the other rider who'd leapt the barriers. This man bore down on him at a gallop.

Cassidy drew and fired his Colt in a single motion, but as the fall from the horse had disorientated him, the shot was wild. As Cassidy aimed more carefully, the rider stood in his saddle and leapt from his horse. The rider grabbed Cassidy around the neck and tumbled them both to the ground in a mountainous cloud of sand.

Cassidy crashed on to his back, the breath blasting from his body. He clawed upward to get his hands around the man's neck, but the sand had clouded his vision and his hands closed on air. Cassidy blinked to clear his eyes.

The man leered down at him. A wave of bad breath filled Cassidy's senses, but, worse, the man held a gun on him.

Cassidy pushed his shoulders down and with a lunge of his hips, he tried to buck the man away.

The man pressed down harder and slipped his

knees upward to pin Cassidy's arms.

Cassidy watched in horror as the man centred the gun on his head. With his teeth gritted, Cassidy waited for the end.

A single gunshot resounded.

The man toppled away.

Behind the dead man stood Graham, a rifle held in his hand. A small plume of smoke wafted from the barrel.

Cassidy pushed the dead man away and rolled to his feet.

'Well done,' he muttered.

Graham gulped, patting his rifle.

'I never shot a man before.'

Normally, Cassidy would sympathize.

'Yeah, but he won't be the last if we get through this.'

Cassidy dashed back to his defensive position.

The riders were no longer before the wagon train circle.

Confused, Cassidy spun around.

Another volley of gunfire sounded as the riders grouped to attack the right-hand side of their circle.

Cassidy dashed around the side of the nearest wagon.

Two pioneers lay sprawled on the ground. Worse, three riders then broke through their defences and grouped inside the circle. One of the riders aimed a rifle down at Graham.

Cassidy charged across the circle. On the run, he fired his Colt twice and the rider tumbled from his horse.

Twenty yards away, Nathaniel struggled with another man, but with the situation desperate, Cassidy could do nothing to help him.

Cassidy dashed to the barriers to search for a way to organize their defence, but none of the pioneers manned the perimeter. They had stopped maintaining the defensive circle. From now on, the fighting would be on an individual level.

Cassidy swirled round.

Pioneers and riders dashed everywhere.

As Cassidy didn't dare fire without a clean target, he dashed for the nearest rider and pulled him from his horse.

The rider tumbled to the ground. As the man tried to get his footing, Cassidy spun him round and clubbed him across the chin with his fist.

With the man stunned, Cassidy glanced around their circle judging who had the upper hand. Each defender was fighting his own battle. Cassidy gulped.

More riders than pioneers were still standing.

Shaking off the hopelessness that threatened to overwhelm him, Cassidy glanced down.

The man was rising, ready to fight back.

Cassidy leapt on the fellow's chest and smashed a fist down into his face.

The man grunted and his head lolled to the side.

A shadow fell across the ground before Cassidy and he glanced up.

Another man had a gun pointed at his chest.

In a desperate lunge, Cassidy leapt for this man's knees as his assailant fired. The gunshot knocked

Cassidy's hat from his head as he tumbled the outlaw down. On his knees, Cassidy gripped his hands together ready to smash them down on the man's stomach, but the man clawed his hands up, getting a grip around Cassidy's neck.

Cassidy thrust his head down. He shrugged the clawing grip away and rolled to the side.

Free for the moment, Cassidy leapt to his feet and scrabbled for his Colt. He pulled it and shot the man through the belly and neck. He moved his gun to the side, looking for more targets, but another man gripped him in a bear-hug from behind.

The unexpected attack knocked Cassidy's Colt to the ground. Cassidy ignored the loss of his weapon and thrust his elbows back into the man's chest. Standing so close, his action had no effect. If anything, the outlaw tightened his grip.

Cassidy pushed his right foot forward and thrust his shoulders down, trying to roll the man over his left shoulder, but the fellow widened his stance and held Cassidy firm.

Then the outlaw he'd pulled from his horse staggered to his feet. He shook his head and grinned at Cassidy.

Cassidy searched for someone who might help, but practically all the pioneers were down. The few left had their own problems.

The outlaw before him pulled his gun, a smirk on his face.

Without a way to dislodge the person who held him, Cassidy thrust out his chest.

'Go on! Kill a sheriff, but you'll regret it.'

The man grinned and instead of firing, glanced around the circle at Vince Chapel's approaching victory.

With the man not killing him, an image of the three skeletons staked somewhere to the north of this battle came to Cassidy. With this terrible thought, Cassidy realized that to satisfy the twisted needs of these men, they'd want some people kept alive.

Cassidy's mind resounded with the thought of such a fate. With a short cry, he thrust all his strength into one lunge. He leapt forward. Simultaneously, he kicked his heels back into the shins of the man behind.

With a pained cry, the fellow collapsed forward on top of him.

They landed heavily, but Cassidy had planned his next move. As the outlaw on top of him oriented, Cassidy pushed his hands downward and with his back flexed, he bucked the man from his back. As soon as the outlaw's grip slipped from his chest, Cassidy slugged him with a solid punch to the jaw.

The man collapsed in a heap and rolled to the side.

Around him, gunfire blasted from the second man. Cassidy ignored the shots. In a rolling leap, he sprang to his feet, but with no control of his direction, he was yards from his Colt.

'Nice move, Sheriff, but not good enough,' the second man muttered, smirking, with his gun on Cassidy.

Cassidy waited for the moment when the outlaw

was prepared to fire. Then he'd try the impossible leap for his Colt, but the impossibility didn't concern Cassidy, he was determined to die while trying to reach his gun. He smiled at the fellow, waiting.

Suddenly, the man stumbled back and fell. A reddened hole was in the middle of his forehead.

'Nice shooting, Nathaniel,' Cassidy mumbled.

He leapt to his Colt and grabbed it. He rolled to his feet and sought his deputy, ready to mount a last stand. As Cassidy turned to the battlefield, another rider fell, and then another. He couldn't see where Nathaniel had positioned himself to create this mayhem. Then he located his deputy on the other side of the circle, wrestling his own assailant.

Cassidy swirled around, searching for whichever pioneer was responsible. Then came another round of gunfire, seemingly from above him. Looking up, he found the source of the gunfire.

Standing fifty feet up, astride the rock, was the man he'd tracked through Hell Creek. The man who had taken the name Matt Travis. His clothes hung from his thin frame, but the sun glinted off the rifle he held in one hand and glinted off the Colt he held in the other. Matt dealt death with each flick of his wrist. Every one of his shots hit its target and those targets were the riders from hell.

Cassidy spun round to see who among their attackers was alive, but after only a few seconds of help from Matt, the only one left was the one fighting with Nathaniel.

Shaking his head in bemusement at their rapid

change of fortunes, Cassidy strode across the circle to the last fight. He slammed a hand on the attacker's back to spin him from Nathaniel.

The man stumbled to the ground, a spreading red bloom coating his forehead.

Cassidy should have been annoyed at this needless death, but in the desperate situation, he didn't mind.

He dashed around the circle and checked the riders from hell, counting a dozen bodies, all dead. Better, he found only three dead pioneers. Although these were three more people than Cassidy wanted to lose, in the circumstances they'd had the luck that he'd prayed to receive.

Most of the pioneers had injuries, but the injuries came from fists not bullets. At first, this annoyed Cassidy. The riders from hell had avoided killing the pioneers. They'd wanted to relive the enjoyment they'd had from torturing Matt Travis's group.

But this was their big mistake. They'd been overconfident and that had given the pioneers, and Matt, the chance they needed.

Accepting that they had won, Cassidy glanced at the rock again.

Matt no longer looked down at them. He stood on a small mound at the base of the rock. As none of the pioneers would approach him, he stood alone.

Cassidy understood the pioneers' problem. They would hate Matt because he'd killed Olivia Smith, but they would be dead if he hadn't helped them. Cassidy held his Colt before him and waited for Matt to walk to him.

Matt swaggered across the circle. When ten yards from Cassidy, he halted and leaned his rifle on his hip.

'Howdy, Sheriff,' he said. 'I'm back. What are you going to do?'

SIXTEEN

As Cassidy couldn't think of an immediate solution for dealing with Matt, he examined the body of the last rider from hell to die.

The sight of the dead man gave Cassidy the answers he needed.

'I suppose I should thank you,' Cassidy said, lowering his Colt.

'Never looked for no thanks. I only wanted to teach the men who destroyed my wagon train that they couldn't get away with that.'

Cassidy nodded toward the swath of bodies around them.

'Looks like you did at that. Seems as though Vince Chapel's riders from hell are staying in Hell Creek.' Cassidy narrowed his eyes. 'This mean you got back your memory?'

'Nope,' Matt said, and smiled. 'Just making an assumption.'

'You assuming that you are Matt Travis is a mighty big assumption. If you're right, it's a pity you could-n't have been so effective on your first trip through

Hell Creek.' Cassidy winced. His comment wasn't subtle.

Matt nodded. 'Yeah, but the outlaws trapped us in the gully. We had no chance. All a man needs is half a chance and in the plains, the odds are more even.'

'With you on our side, the odds favoured us.'

'Leaves you with a problem, Sheriff. What will you do with me?'

Cassidy ran a hand over his sweating brow.

'What would you suggest?'

Moving his hand with deliberate slowness, Matt laid his rifle on the ground. Then using only his thumb and forefinger, he pulled his Colt from its holster and laid it in his left hand.

Cassidy nodded at the gun.

'Does that mean you're giving yourself up?'

'I got the justice I was looking for here and helped another wagon train, but that don't excuse what I done to Olivia Smith.'

In his time as a lawman, Cassidy couldn't remember a single occasion when a wrongdoer had given himself up without good cause. Confused as to how he should respond, Cassidy lifted his hat and scratched his head.

'The way I see it, I don't know what you did to Olivia Smith, or what your reasons were. Before I decide what I'll do with you, you've earned the right to tell me your side of the story.'

Matt shrugged. 'The only person who can give the full story is dead and buried.'

'Maybe, but as a lawman, I can tell the difference between the truth and lies, so tell me.'

In truth, as a poker-player, Cassidy only knew when men were hiding something, but Matt didn't need to know that.

Matt stared at his gun.

'When you left us near my wagon train, Olivia pulled a rifle on me,' he said with his voice low. 'She said a lot of things, none of which made sense to a man who wasn't sure of his own name, but from what she said, I used to know her. I also reckon I'd done wrong by her and she hadn't taken too kindly to that.'

'What do you think you did to her in the past?'

'No idea, but there's several possibilities, none of which show me in a good light. Anyhow, she was mighty annoyed and I was sure she'd turn the rifle on me, but no use wondering about that. The result was I'm alive and she's dead. Ain't a man alive who can be happy about that.'

Cassidy accepted Matt's answer. This might not be the full truth, but, in this situation, obtaining the proof for proper justice was impossible. Cassidy believed you judged a man by his actions more than any other way. After what he'd done, Matt deserved leeway.

Cassidy holstered his own Colt.

'Put your gun away. I won't take it.'

With a quick touch of his right hand to his hat, Matt nodded.

'I owe you a debt. Not many men would side with me.'

Of this, Cassidy was sure.

'I ain't doing you that big a favour. The way I see it, I can't know whether you killed Olivia Smith in self-defence or for some another reason, but one man reckons he knows the answer. When he finds you, he'll ask you that question and you'll need to be mighty convincing.'

'Burton Smith,' Matt whispered. With a whirl of his hand, he thrust the Colt back in its holster. 'Reckon as you're right at that.'

Cassidy nodded at the wagon train, where Graham Wainwright was organizing his people into a burial duty for the dead riders. Cassidy wouldn't have bothered.

'You joining them to look for a new life in California? If you are Matt Travis that's where you were heading before.'

With a sigh, Matt shook his head.

'Nope. I don't know these people and I don't reckon they want to know me. I might go West one day, but not today. If it's the same with you, I'll feed and water my horse and head back to Hell's End, and who knows what afterwards.'

Cassidy nodded.

With a short returning nod, Matt picked up his rifle and wandered to his horse.

'Are you sure about that, Cassidy?' Nathaniel said when they were alone. 'We were lucky he rescued us from this attack, but he killed a woman.'

'I know, but Burton Smith returned to Hell's End to wait for him and whatever the truth is will kind of resolve itself before nightfall.'

'Matt is handy with a gun. Burton might not be a match for him.'

Cassidy shook his head.

'I never trusted Burton Smith. There's more to him than he shows. It'll be a fair fight.'

'Ain't you telling Matt that Burton's waiting for him in Hell's End?'

'Nope, ain't siding with either Matt Travis or Burton Smith.'

Nathaniel smiled. 'In that, I can agree.'

Cassidy turned to practical concerns. He pointed at the wagons.

'Ensure Graham doesn't waste time burying those riders. Burying his people is fine, but Vince Chapel's riders from hell only deserve to feed the vultures. We're behind schedule and I don't want to spend the rest of my life in Hell Creek.'

Nathaniel nodded and strode to Graham.

While everyone bustled, Cassidy decided to ensure the wagon train was operational. First, he strode to the table that had taken the brunt of the bullets at the start of the fight and wondered if the heavily holed wood was worth taking with them.

Someone coughed.

Cassidy glanced up.

Matt was on his horse and ready to travel back to Hell's End. He sat sideways, the lowering sun at his back.

'I'll be saying goodbye to you then, Sheriff.'

With one hand shading his eyes from the sun, Cassidy nodded.

'Good luck. Maybe I'll see you again one day. I hope by then that you'll have your memory back, and you'll know who you really are and what you were doing here.'

'Me too, but I've pieced together enough of my memory to know that Burton Smith won't succeed in ambushing me at Hell's End.'

Matt tipped his hat and pulled his horse away.

'How did you know Burton would be there?' Cassidy shouted as Matt trotted from the circle.

'Because that's where I'd be,' Matt muttered without looking back.

Matt galloped away, his horse's hoofs sending vast plumes of sand into the swirling breeze. Quicker than Cassidy expected, the rider disappeared into the haze-filled desert.

Cassidy tore his gaze from the desert to concentrate on the task ahead, but Nathaniel strode to him, his jaw set firm. Accepting he was about to hear bad news, Cassidy nodded to his deputy.

'What's wrong?'

'I've examined the riders' bodies. You'd better come look at them.'

Nathaniel spun round.

With his curiosity piqued, Cassidy followed his deputy.

Fifty yards from the wagon train, the pioneers had laid the twelve bodies in a row. Cassidy leaned over the first body and saw what worried his deputy.

'That's the storekeeper at Hell's End, isn't it?'

Nathaniel nodded. 'Sure is.'

'Didn't notice the likeness before, but I suppose I was too busy fighting for my life and not looking for people I recognized.'

'That's not all. Another one of these men was in the saloon when we arrived in Hell's End. Another man is Gordon, the man who claimed to be the town's mayor.'

Graham joined them in examining the bodies. Cassidy considered each rider, wondering which body might be Vince Chapel's. With no clues, the leader's identity would probably remain a mystery.

'I've asked around,' Graham said, 'and we recognize most of them as being men from Hell's End. Looks like these bodies ain't Vince Chapel's riders from hell but are the townsfolk of Hell's End.'

Nathaniel shook his head.

'Nope, this fits in with some other things I saw. A big graveyard was outside Hell's End. I reckon Vince's riders from hell were pretending to be the townsfolk. The real ones are long dead.'

While rubbing the back of his neck, Graham whistled.

'We should thank you for what you did, Sheriff, but this only proves I was right all along. We were safer leaving Hell's End. I never liked that place.' Graham smiled. 'But we got them all. Nobody else will suffer at their hands.'

Cassidy considered how many townsfolk he'd seen in Hell's End. He shook his head.

'Don't reckon we got the whole town. Could be more of them than we have here.'

Graham shrugged. 'Don't reckon those that are left will have much fight left in them to take on other innocent travellers.'

Cassidy nodded. He glanced eastward. There, the cloud of sand from Matt's hurried departure had blown away.

'Maybe whoever is left won't take on the innocent travellers,' Cassidy muttered with his hands on his hips, 'but the guilty ones might not fare so well.'

SEVENTEEN

Riding from Hell Creek, Matt Travis approached Hell's End. Now he would resolve his life. He may not have a past, but he only cared about his immediate future.

He expected that the remaining townsfolk of Hell's End would be interested in his arrival, so he rode around the edge of town and reined his horse at the back of the stable.

With his rifle slung over one shoulder, Matt debated whether to continue his sneaked approach to Hell's End. But he had no reason to come crawling back. From now on, Matt Travis wouldn't sneak and hide.

He swaggered around the stable and strode to the centre of the road.

The sun was low in the sky. The huge flattened orb turned red as it blasted the last of its heat down on the hard ground.

Matt strode down the road. His long shadow lay before him as he headed towards the saloon. He'd decided that Burton Smith would be waiting for him there.

That's where Matt would wait.

Matt swaggered to a halt in the doorway. This was when he was at his most vulnerable. The sun had dazzled him and the darkness within the saloon was absolute. But by killing him here, a man who wanted revenge wouldn't get the satisfaction he sought.

Showing he had no fear, Matt waited for long moments. In the shade, the flies buzzed. When his gaze discerned objects within the saloon, he pushed open the swing doors and swaggered inside to stand two paces before the door.

Four men he didn't recognize were inside. They leaned against the back wall. With fingers hooked into their gunbelts, they cocked their hats downward, partially hiding their cold eyes, which were nestled in a swath of dirt and bristles. None of the men was Burton Smith.

Matt nodded to them.

'I've come to see Burton Smith,' he muttered through clenched teeth.

The man at the end chuckled deep in his throat.

'Who might he be?'

Matt saw no reason to waste time discussing why he was here.

'He's the man I'm here to see.'

The man spat a long stream of spittle on to the floor.

'Who is here to see him?'

'That depends on who's asking the question,' Matt whispered, grinning.

The man pushed from the wall. His three companions matched the action.

'You ain't being friendly for a stranger. Answer the question. Who are you?'

Although he'd fought to regain the pieces of his memory that he possessed, Matt saw no reason to explain that to these men. He was only interested in Burton Smith. If they wanted a fight before he met him, he'd oblige.

'My name ain't important to you, Vince Chapel.'

All four men laughed aloud at that comment, slapping their thighs in exaggerated mirth. Then as one, their chuckling died, and the first man set his mouth back to the previous sneer.

'Burton was right. You ain't got any memory left.'

Matt dismissed this mistake from his thoughts.

'I remember enough.'

'Doubt it. If you did, you'd sure remember your meeting with Vince Chapel.'

A chuckle came from within the shadows of the only side door.

Matt turned to the door.

From the shadows, Burton Smith emerged.

'Wiley here is right,' he said. 'You should remember meeting Vince Chapel. Except the reason that you can't remember anything is down to what Vince did to Matt Travis's wagon train.'

Matt smiled. 'That victory didn't do Vince much good. Vince suffered the inevitable end all outlaws suffer. He met people who organized themselves better than he organized his own men. Vince couldn't have been too good, because Graham Wainwright's motley group of pioneers saw him off. Vince is lying dead in Hell Creek with the rest of his riders from hell.'

The man on the left snorted.

'Doubt that,' Burton said.

Matt grinned. 'Stay ignorant then, but you'll wait for them to return for ever. You see, all on my own I've figured out that when the riders don't return you'll need someone else to run the saloon and stores, even to be town mayor.'

Burton Smith hunched his shoulders.

'Figured that out on your own, did you? It don't matter none. Vince Chapel's end was inevitable. He killed Frank Chapel for more power, but before long, someone else with better ideas would arrive.'

'I presume that Burton Smith has the better ideas,' Matt muttered with dawning realization of what was happening here.

'Frank and Vince only knew how to kill, but the man before you knows how to think, how to plan, and more important, how to win.'

Dismissing the infighting of men he didn't know or want to know, from his mind, Matt knew everyone in this room was against him.

From the corner of his eye, Matt judged the distance to the four outlaws and Burton Smith, choosing which one he'd kill first. He doubted he'd have the time to kill five men before one of them stopped him, but he'd die trying.

As Matt prepared his onslaught, footsteps sounded in the road. Without turning, he knew that his small chance had gone. Matt nodded to Burton and spread his hands wide.

'Looks like you got me.'

Burton widened his grin. 'Sure does.'

With his head to one side, Matt listened. The footsteps paced across the porch. Three men were outside, presumably with their guns drawn and centred on his back.

Without looking back, Matt strode forward a pace, allowing the men to slip through the swing-doors. Matt hoped that when they filed through the entrance the men would be confident and off guard. Then he'd make his move.

The swing-doors creaked as the first man pushed into the saloon.

While keeping his expression resigned, Matt transferred his weight to his left leg ready to dive for the floor.

'Who's he?' someone shouted, outside.

Matt didn't pause to wonder what the confusion was. He dropped to the floor, skidding along the sand-strewn timbers to roll on his back. He spun his rifle to his shoulder and took the man in the doorway through the belly, low and deadly.

Matt dropped the rifle. He slipped his Colt from its holster and swung it towards the men at the back wall. Gunshots blasted around him and outside. He hit two men in high shots to the head and neck.

The other men dropped to the floor.

Matt scrambled along the floor and leapt behind a table. This would give him scant cover, but enough while he oriented himself. He peered over the top of the table.

Burton ran from the saloon through the side door.

Running crouched, the other two men dashed after him.

Matt ignored them. He swung round. The front doorway was clear, the swing-doors creaking back and forth. He leapt to his feet and dashed past the body in the doorway and into the road.

Outside, two other men lay sprawled on the ground, blood coating their chests. But Matt kept his gaze on the sole man surviving, who crouched in the road, his Colt held at arm's length as he stared down the road.

'Sheriff.'

'Matt.'

'You returned. I thought you'd let me seek my fate on my own?'

Cassidy tipped his hat.

'Glad to do that when I thought this was about you and Burton Smith. Then I discovered that the outlaws ran this town and I returned to finish what you'd started back at the wagon train.'

'Glad to hear it. Where's your deputy?'

With a quick glance down the road, Sheriff Cassidy dashed across the road to him.

'I left him to guard the wagon train,' he whispered, 'but no need to let everyone else know that. How many are we facing?'

'Aside from the dead ones, I saw Burton and two others.'

'Burton Smith is alive?' Cassidy said, with his eyebrows raised. 'Thought they'd kill him as soon as he returned.'

Matt sighed. The sheriff was intelligent enough to

work out some of what had happened here, but he hadn't figured out how Burton Smith fitted into the set-up. Matt wasn't too sure either, but he kept his thoughts private.

'Sure looks that way. What do you want to do?'

'You worry about Burton. The other men are my responsibility.'

Nodding, Matt turned from Cassidy to look down the road. Close to the saloon, they were far enough away from the other side of the road to be safe from all but the expert gunfighter. Anyone hiding on their side was more of a concern.

A few yards apart, they strode past the saloon, Colts drawn and ready for the inevitable attack. Matt ran his gaze along the buildings on his side of the road and then, ten yards ahead, a rifle poked around the corner of the stores.

A shot blasted and the rifle flew away, Cassidy hitting the weapon with one shot.

A man leapt from beside the stores and dashed two paces.

Cassidy took the man through the stomach.

The man collapsed face down.

'Nice shooting,' Matt muttered.

A timber creaked. Matt swirled round.

Two men slipped past the side of the saloon.

Matt fired twice but, on the turn, his shots went wild, clattering into the wall beside the men.

The men leapt into the road, rolling as they went. On their bellies, they fired up at Matt.

Gunshots hurtled by Matt's head. With longer to aim, he fired twice, blasting each man in the shoulders.

The men cried out and dropped their rifles.

Matt swirled round, searching for anyone else who might leap out, but the road remained empty.

As Matt waited, Cassidy dashed to the fallen men. He kicked their rifles away, then pulled their guns from their holsters and tossed them over his shoulder.

'If you live, you is under arrest. If you die, you is still under arrest,' Cassidy muttered, staring down at them. 'Tell me how many more are with you.'

The nearest man gasped through clenched teeth.

'No way we're talking, Sheriff.'

Cassidy turned back to Matt.

'What do you reckon? Do we have all of Vince's riders from hell?'

Matt shrugged as he reloaded his gun.

'We already have one more than I reckoned was here. Can't know yet whether your job is complete.'

'Correction,' a voice from beside the saloon muttered.

Matt spun round.

Burton stepped into the fading sunlight.

'The sheriff's job is complete, but Matt and I have unfinished business.'

Matt glared at Burton.

While flexing his hand, Burton glared back at him.

With his eyes narrowed, Matt waited for the telltale twitch of Burton's arm.

'I'm here and ready to sort this,' Matt whispered, 'so what are you waiting for?'

Burton smiled, grimly. 'I'm making sure that this fight ain't two against one before I make my move.'

'I'm afraid it is,' Sheriff Cassidy said.

Matt swung to the side, but kept Burton in his sights. From the corner of his eye, he saw that the sheriff had his Colt drawn.

'Why is your gun drawn, Cassidy?' Matt muttered, backing a pace. 'This is between Burton and me. This ain't your fight.'

Cassidy shook his head.

'This *is* my fight, and this fight *is* about two men against one man. Except the one man is you, Matt. You killed Olivia Smith in cold blood and perhaps you did a lot more besides. I'm a lawman and I can't ignore that.'

Matt accepted that Cassidy had now picked his side, so he considered his chances. From what he'd seen of his own gunfighting in the last day, he might be quick enough to take either of these men, perhaps both, but not when one man had already pulled his gun.

'Stay away, Cassidy. This has nothing to do with you. Don't force me to kill you.'

'Matt is right,' Burton muttered to Matt's surprise. 'This has nothing to do with you, Cassidy. This is between Matt and me. The law don't figure in our dispute.'

Matt grinned and turned to square off to Burton.

Cassidy cocked his gun.

'So, we're in agreement,' the sheriff said. 'Your fight has nothing to do with me. You, Burton, have the right to kill Matt for killing your woman, but if Matt kills you, that'll be the last thing he does. I promised you that in Hell Creek and I forgot that for a while, but I'm back here to complete my promise.'

Matt glanced at the gun and at the sheriff holding the gun. Nothing from either suggested he'd live if he killed Burton. He shook his head.

'Sheriff, you ain't worked out what's happening here, have you?'

Cassidy shrugged without moving the gun aimed at Matt.

'Don't care who you are, Matt, or what you've done. All I know is that you killed Olivia Smith and any man that kills a woman deserves to die.'

'That's a change, Cassidy. Before, you were prepared to give me the benefit of the doubt.'

'Then, I'd kind of forgot the promise I made to Burton and I hate doing that. You can sort out your differences with him, but you don't get to leave Hell's End. I don't reckon you *are* Matt Travis, but even so, I'll put the name Matt Travis on your grave.'

Matt considered. He smiled.

'And what name will you put on Burton Smith's grave?'

Burton laughed. 'Who says I'll die?'

Keeping his actions slow, Matt held his arms wide. The sheriff needed to know the truth before he acted on an old promise.

'Everyone dies some day, but do you think people will grieve over Burton Smith or over Tom Tinbrush from my old wagon train? Those men have different names, but they use the same letters and, more importantly, they're the same person.'

'What?' Cassidy shouted, moving his Colt from Matt to Burton.

Matt coughed. 'I have more, Sheriff. Do you reckon Burton Smith shed tears over the grave of Olivia Smith or over the grave of Sarah Tinbrush? Different names, different letters, but the same woman.'

Burton shrugged. 'I've no idea what Matt means.'

Cassidy shook his head.

'No, you know what Matt means. When Matt killed Olivia, you said Sarah's name. How can they be the same person?'

'Don't listen to this madman,' Burton muttered. 'He's been in the sun too long. His memory is fried.'

Matt's memory would never recover, but he had pieced together a few assumptions.

'I reckon I am Matt Travis. I led a wagon train to California and two of my pioneers were Tom and Sarah Tinbrush. They directed our route across Hell Creek to the ambush they'd arranged with Frank Chapel. Afterwards, Tom and Sarah joined the next wagon train posing as Burton and Olivia Smith. They planned to lead it into the same trap as they'd done with the other missing wagon trains. Except by then, Vince Chapel organized the ambush. Vince is dead too now and Burton Smith is the last of the riders from hell, but he's planning how he'll organize another gang and another ambush.'

Burton chuckled and spread his hands wide.

'Sounds a wild theory to me, with no proof.'

With his free hand, Cassidy rubbed his brow, nodding. He turned to Burton.

'Except Matt saw you rummaging through the clothing of one of the bodies by the wagon train.

You're the one who claimed to have found Tom Tinbrush's body.'

'If I did that, why didn't I pretend to find Sarah Tinbrush's body too?'

As Cassidy rubbed his brow, Matt smiled. This was easy to understand.

'I reckon Burton wanted to distract our trusty lawmen into searching for a woman they could never find while the riders from hell took Graham's wagon train.'

Cassidy turned his gun from Burton. With a short whirl of his arm, he thrust his Colt back in its holster.

'What are you doing?' Burton muttered.

Frowning, Cassidy tipped his hat.

'I'm saying goodbye to you. The way I see this, I don't know which one of you is telling the truth, because both of you are hiding something. Except I don't know what it is. Matt, if that's who you are, you don't have enough rational thought left to be guilty of your crime. Burton, you've never been straight with me, so my promise to you means nothing.'

'Go then,' Burton whispered.

Cassidy nodded. 'I'll do what I intended to do before. I'll leave you to decide who is right and who is wrong. I have a wagon train that needs escorting to California. Night's a-coming and I'm more than ready to leave Hell.'

'Thanks, Cassidy,' Matt said in genuine gratitude. 'You've decided right.'

'Just remember, I won't take kindly to seeing either of you again,' Cassidy muttered. With a contemptuous sneer, he turned from them. 'To my way of thinking, the only right result will be if you kill each other.'

The lawman strode down the road. From the corner of his eye, he glanced at the two men lying on the ground.

'Reckon as you two ain't under arrest any more. If you live, stay out of my sight too.'

Cassidy tipped his hat and strode down the centre of the road. Beyond the final building, he disappeared into a heat haze.

Then the only sound in Hell's End was the buzzing of flies nearby.

Matt turned to Burton. He paced to his left to avoid staring into the huge red orb of the setting sun.

The first cooling breeze of the day blew down the road, rustling the sand around Matt's feet.

'Just you and me now, Burton.'

Burton shuffled down and leaned forward.

'Suppose I wouldn't have it any other way.'

With a sigh, Matt wondered from where his confidence sprang. He wiped the sweat from his forehead. With the gesture, he glanced to his left and right, confirming that nobody else was close. As he turned his gaze back, Burton glanced to Matt's right.

Matt smiled. Somebody else with a gun was on this road and he now knew where he was.

Burton shuffled his feet further apart and blew on his right hand.

'Before I kill you, shall I tell you the truth about what we did to you back at that wagon train? The things that force a man to forget, just to keep his sanity.'

'Nothing you could say would interest me.'

'Not even the truth about who you were before the sun fried what was left of your mind?'

'You'll take that knowledge to the grave.'

'Fine by me,' Burton muttered, grinning.

Burton lowered his shoulder.

Matt leapt to his right. He landed on his side and fired up at Burton. He didn't wait to discover if he'd hit him, but rolled to his side as an explosion of gunfire ripped into the ground beside him. He rolled twice then searched for the hidden assailant across the road. He faced two more men.

With a casual flick of his hand, Matt put a bullet in the first man's shoulder from thirty yards, and two more through the legs of the second man.

Matt jumped to his feet to face Burton. As he had thought, he'd hit Burton in the right hand.

Burton knelt on the ground, edging his left hand towards his gun, which lay before him.

'Go on,' Matt said, smiling. 'You can take the gun.'

With an ungainly juggle, Burton snatched the gun with his left hand. In his unfamiliar grip, Burton held the gun awkwardly. He pushed to his feet.

Matt thrust his Colt back into its holster and spread his arms.

'Burton, I'll give you more of a chance than you'd give me. You can have one shot at me with your left hand. If you miss me, I'll kill you. If you hit me, you get to live.'

Burton wrung his bleeding right hand and shuffled the gun further into his left hand.

'With your ruined memory, how do you know I

can't shoot well with my left hand?'

Matt nodded at Burton's hand.

'I ain't got much of a memory, but I recognize gun skills. You've never used that hand before.'

Burton chuckled. 'You're right at that, but why give me the opportunity? I'd never give you the same chance.'

'I killed Sarah Tinbrush and Olivia Smith with one rifle shot. They were two women that you loved. In the circumstance, I suppose I ought to give you a chance.'

Burton spat on the ground.

'For your information, in case I miss you, the name of the woman you killed wasn't Olivia Smith or Sarah Tinbrush. They were aliases she used. Her full name was Matilda Sarah Smith, except I used to call her Sarah.' Burton narrowed his eyes. 'Others called her Mattie.'

Matt considered. 'Don't seem important.'

'Suppose it don't any more.'

Burton lifted his left arm, holding the gun at arm's length. The arm was steady, but the gun shook in his hand.

Matt waited until Burton had the gun almost steady. Then Matt whirled his arm. With his Colt in his hand, he shot the gun from Burton's hand.

With his face set in a grimace of pain, Burton staggered back and fell to his knees, his left hand thrust beneath his armpit.

'I thought you said you'd give me a chance,' Burton muttered through pained gasps.

Matt whirled his arm to slip his Colt back in its holster and smiled.

'I lied. Something you'd know all about.'

Matt sauntered forward. He grabbed Burton's gun from the ground and swaggered in an arc down the road. With the sun having set, the ground darkened as Matt loomed over the first of the surviving riders from hell.

The man writhed on the ground clutching his shoulder, but with only a smattering of blood on him; he'd live.

Matt smiled at him.

The second man also lay on his back, blood welling down his arm; but again, he'd live.

Matt smiled at him too.

He strode across the road to the other two men he'd shot.

The third man lay with his hands grasping his legs. Thick blood seeped through his fingers.

Matt frowned. He drew his Colt and shot the man in the forehead.

The fourth man looked up at him, with his chin thrust forward as he prepared to die.

Matt confirmed that this man only had a gunshot to the shoulder. He favoured him with another wide smile and shook his head.

'Sorry, you ain't so lucky. You get to live.'

'What are you doing?' Burton shouted from across the road, his hands held outstretched and thick with blood.

Standing in the middle of Hell's End, Matt threw back his head and laughed aloud. He wandered back across the road and stared down at Burton.

'I think you know what will happen next,' he

muttered with his voice low. 'For what I am about to do, I only need three live men and you, Burton Smith.'

Matt glanced over his shoulder at the stores, hoping he'd find everything that he needed there. He only needed a few yards of rope, sixteen stakes and a sharp knife.

The desert would do the rest.

EIGHTEEN

The vultures were closer now.

In an unending barrage, the sun beat down its merciless heat on to the rock-filled Utah desert.

Beneath the inferno, a man lay spread-eagled, facing upward. The sun's rays blistered the staked man's fried skin. Without water for days, his throat was a barren wasteland. He tried to move his arms, but the stakes holding his limbs were as solid as ever.

To avoid looking at the sun, the staked man stretched his neck as far as possible and stared down the road. Before him were three other men, also staked in the middle of the road. The vultures squabbled over them.

From these men's prolonged screaming two days ago, the staked man knew they were dead. Their method of dying was terrible but he envied them.

They didn't suffer this living hell.

The staked man closed his eyes and his head fell back to the ground. He prayed for the first time in his life, but prayed that death would come soon. Around the man, the huge birds flapped. The beating of wings masked the droning buzz of flies.

From somewhere, an acrid burning odour emerged. He rolled his head to the right.

Flames licked around the saloon doorway.

Without much interest, the staked man watched the flames. He was aware that fire was a problem, but unless the flames crossed the hard road, they wouldn't end his life.

The flames grew, sending plumes of black smoke spiralling into the blue sky. Crackling echoed and with the thick smoke, the staked man coughed, but his throat was too dry to relieve the stinging.

He turned his head from the flames. A stray spark must have reached the other side of the road. A roaring inferno ripped across the stable's dry timbers.

The staked man closed his dry eyes to protect them from the smoke and lay back. Crackling sounds surrounded him. The fire intensified the baking heat of the day to an unbearable level.

If the staked man had enough moisture left in his body to sweat, the heat would dry his skin in seconds.

Without warning, a cooling shadow fell across the staked man's face.

The blissful release was a short-lived pleasure. The shadow would come from a vulture that was brave enough to risk the fire to feed.

Within the staked man, there beat a tortured desire for life. He opened his eyes and cried soundlessly at the vulture.

The shadow wasn't from a vulture. A man loomed over him. The fire at his back etched his thin body in sharp relief.

The staked man couldn't remember who had staked him here, why he was here, or even what his own name was. This was irrelevant now. Help had come.

'Help me,' the staked man said. Only a croak slipped from his blistered lips.

From above, a sun-halo surrounded the looming man's face, the glow flickering as swathes of smoke plumed behind him. A broad smile gleamed down at the staked man.

'Afternoon, Burton Smith. You look warm.'

Burton sighed, drily. He mumbled his name. The simple pleasure at remembering who he was filled his mind.

This man's voice sounded familiar too, but Burton didn't care, he had an identity of his own.

Putting all his effort into making his throat work, Burton uttered a few words. A croaking emerged from his body, as rusty as an old locomotive.

'Get me out of here, please.'

The man shook his head. 'You are going nowhere.'

The man turned and paced from view.

With the sun again blasting down on him, Burton licked a rasping tongue around his mouth, but he failed to generate any moisture.

'You can't leave me,' he croaked.

'Sure can,' the man said, standing away from Burton's line of sight. Footsteps echoed on the hard ground as the man strode away. Leather creaked when the man leapt into a saddle. The horse clumped into view. Then blocking the sun, the man glanced at the burning buildings, nodding to each in turn.

'Go to hell,' Burton muttered.

The man looked down at Burton from on high, grinning.

'I ain't going to hell,' he muttered, surrounded with smoke. 'Hell is where I've been and hell is where you're staying.'

Although Burton knew his own name now, he was too weak to remember anything else.

'Who are you?' Burton whispered as the rider turned away.

The man paused. He stared down the burning road.

'You didn't give me the dignity of dying, knowing who I was or why I was dying, but I lived and learned the truth. Now you can die instead, but I'll give you a choice. Do you want me to tell you the truth or do you want to die in ignorance?'

'Please tell me,' Burton whispered, with nothing left to live for.

The man nodded. 'I've learnt that I led a wagon train through Hell's End and the town you helped run ambushed us. You thought you'd killed everyone, but you didn't win because I lived. I killed your woman. I killed your men. And I destroyed your town. You're the last of the riders from hell. Now I'm returning to Beaver Ridge. Later, I'll bring another wagon train through Hell Creek, but with Hell's End dead, we'll succeed. If you're lucky, I'll bury any of your bones that the vultures leave.'

Burton considered this statement, remembering

some of the events the man described. He had only one final question.

'And what's your name?'

The man stared at the burning buildings.

'The name's Matt Travis.'

Now Burton remembered everything that had happened. Risking his lips cracking apart, he smiled.

With a tip of his hat, Matt Travis pulled his horse away. The hoof-beats receded down the road.

Burton lifted his head as far as he could.

Through the swirling curtains of black smoke, Matt Travis rode from Burton Smith. His hunched form disappeared into fragmented heat-shimmers on the edge of Hell's End.

Now Burton Smith was alone.

Burton Smith smiled some more as he allowed this alias, along with his other aliases, to die. With death close, he concentrated on his real identity: his given name of Vince Chapel.

Vince lay back. The smoke plumed into the sky above him.

Vince Chapel savoured his last moments of existence and his final victory. He knew he'd die with his identity intact, which was something his killer would probably never earn.

Vince's smile widened.

'You're wrong, Frank,' Vince Chapel croaked to the departed rider. 'I ain't the last rider from hell. When you reach Beaver Ridge, I hope Marshal Devine gives you a good reception.'

Vince Chapel laughed.

The bone-dry rattle from Vince's shrunken body

drifted down the smoky road. The sound joined the flies and the heat as it filled the burning Hell's End.

Only the approaching vultures heard him.